JULIA AND THE HAND OF GOD

Whenever Julia Redfern went to meet Uncle Hugh in San
Francisco, she thought of earthquakes, and the day of her
eleventh birthday was no exception. In the midst of the
elegant lunch, she had to hear once again the story of how
he survived what her grandmother had called, "the Hand
of God laying low the wicked city." That was the lunch at
which Hugh presented her with the richly bound volume
of blank pages for her to fill—her Book of Strangenesses.
And this is the story of all the sad, funny, and wonderfully
wild happenings that go into Julia's book.

"Cameron succeeds in bringing readers directly into Julia's
world."

—*School Library Journal* (Starred review)

PUFFIN BOOKS BY ELEANOR CAMERON

Julia's Magic
That Julia Redfern
Julia and the Hand of God
A Room Made of Windows
The Private Worlds of Julia Redfern

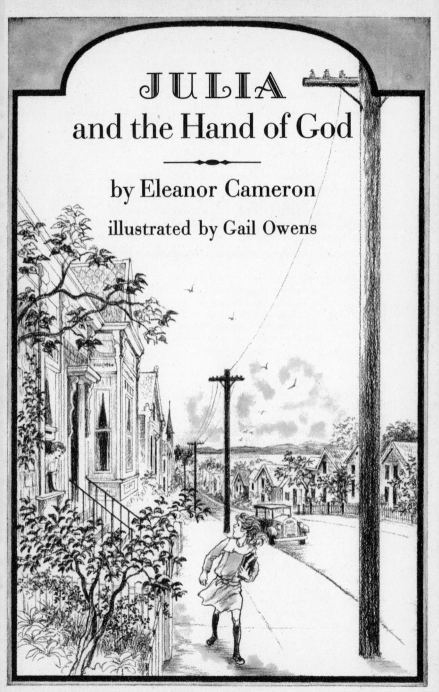

JULIA
and the Hand of God

by Eleanor Cameron

illustrated by Gail Owens

Puffin Books

PUFFIN BOOKS

Published by the Penguin Group

Viking Penguin Group

Viking Penguin, a division of Penguin Books USA Inc.,
40 West 23rd Street, New York, New York 10010, U.S.A.

Penguin Books Ltd, 27 Wrights Lane, London W8 5TZ, England

Penguin Books Australia Ltd, Ringwood, Victoria, Australia

Penguin Books Canada Ltd, 2801 John Street, Markham, Ontario, Canada L3R 1B4

Penguin Books (N.Z.) Ltd, 182–190 Wairau Road, Auckland 10, New Zealand

Penguin Book Ltd, Registered Offices: Harmondsworth, Middlesex, England

First published in the United States of America by E. P. Dutton,
a division of Penguin Books USA Inc., 1977
Published in Puffin Books 1989
1 3 5 7 9 10 8 6 4 2
Text copyright © Eleanor Cameron, 1977
Illustrations copyright © Gail Owens, 1977
All rights reserved

LIBRARY OF CONGRESS CATALOGING-IN-PUBLICATION DATA

Cameron, Eleanor, 1912–

Julia and the hand of God / by Eleanor Cameron ; illustrated by Gail Owens.   p.   cm.

Sequel: A room made of windows.

Sequel to: That Julia Redfern.

Summary: A series of crises lead eleven-year-old Julia to see her family
in a different light and help her reaffirm her ambition to be a writer

ISBN 0 14 034042 4

[1. Family life—Fiction.]   I. Owens, Gail, ill.   II. Title.

[PZ7.C143Ju   1989]   [Fic]—dc19   89-30230

Printed in the United States of America
By R. R. Donnelley & Sons Company, Harrisonburg, Virginia
Set in Caledonia

Except in the United States of America, this book is sold subject to the
condition that it shall not, by way of trade or otherwise, be lent,
re-sold, hired out, or otherwise circulated without the publisher's prior
consent in any form of binding or cover other than that in which it is
published and without a similar condition including this condition being
imposed on the subsequent purchaser.

For Phyllis
and David—
each knows why

Contents

1

———◆———

Seeing Things

Julia's birthday, and they were on the train from Berkeley headed for the Oakland Mole where the ferry came
that would take them across the bay to San Francisco to
meet Uncle Hugh at the Green Door. It was terribly expensive to have lunch there. They never went, she and
Mama and Greg, except when Uncle Hugh, who was rich,
took them on special occasions like birthdays, or Easter,
or the first Sunday after the last day of school.

Julia sat by the train window making up conversa-
tions while the Southern Pacific slid through the out-
skirts of Oakland toward Shellmound Park with rich,
heavy clicks of its wheels as it rolled over the track joints.
She couldn't begin to imagine why Shellmound was
called a park. When you got there, it stank with all sorts
of things lying around rotting on the shores of the bay
in the hot sun, and there were mounds and mounds of

old shells. But at the moment Julia wasn't noticing where they were. Seeing herself and Mama and Greg going along the street in San Francisco, she thought of earthquakes.

Always, when they went across to the city to shop or go to the park and the museum, she had a moment of freezing, almost ecstatic terror the second they stepped off the ferry, that now, right now, on this particular day they'd chosen to come, would be the day of the next earthquake. Uncle Hugh and Aunt Alex had been through the last one, years and years ago before they were married, the one that had leveled Aunt Alex's home to the ground.

Julia's eyes widened, she stared across at Greg sitting opposite her, reading one of his everlasting Egyptian books. Mama was beside her, but all at once they might just as well not have been there.

She was looking out over San Francisco, tottering, shaking, tumbling to pieces. She smelled gas. There was a continuous rending and crashing. She heard people screaming, saw them running—but where could they go? It made no difference where they went. No, you could run and run, but the terrible rumbling coming up from the bowels of the earth would keep right on, and buildings would disappear into chasms that opened before your very eyes the way they had Uncle Hugh's. And you would turn and run in the other direction, only to have a building rain its bricks on you, or cornices weighing tons, with the whole side of it swaying out and hanging over your head—

Julia gave a gasp and put her hands up to her face.

2

She was standing on a hill, for some reason, behind women with big hats and long dark skirts. But at the same time she was running—now here, now there—wildly, like some mindless, frantic animal with its heart beating so hard it could scarcely—

"Julia! Stop it—stop it this instant!" It was a low, urgent, private voice right above her head, and Mama was leaning close and had put her hand on Julia's knee, grasping it and giving it a shake. "Stop it at once. How many times must I tell you not to do that! People will think you're mad." Julia gulped in her breath and looked up.

"What was I doing?" It was as if she'd come out of a trance.

"Staring, the way you always do in that awful way. What on earth do you see, Julia? Why do you persist in doing it?"

"But I can't help it. I've told you a million times—I've *told* you. I don't try—it just happens. I'm thinking about something and then all of a sudden—it's there."

"What was there?"

Julia looked down, her mouth set in that stubborn line she could feel. Then she darted a glance up at Greg. He was studying her.

"You're an absurd creature, Jule Redfern," he said, and he pushed his glasses up on his beak of a nose with a flick of his finger. But there was a certain light in his eye that she knew very well. He was on her side, and she bet anything he did it too—saw things, saw the Egyptian tombs with their dank, moldering, thousands-of-centuries dead mummies, felt himself stealing along some black, deafeningly silent passageway, maybe on his hands and knees, all alone, knowing he would be cursed forever for it. Maybe die the next year of some horrible, lingering disease. She gave him a quick wink.

The only thing about Greg was, if he *did* do it—see things as if they were real and happening—he'd be clever enough not to let anyone know, with his head lowered over his book. Oh, he was a clever one. Not like her stupid self who did everything right out, so that Gramma was always shrieking at her that she filled the whole house with her moods and her doings. ("Your grandmother never shrieks, Julia. Why must you exaggerate?")

"*What* was there?" It was Mama, still wanting to know.

"Nothing. I won't tell—it's private. Can't *any*thing be private?" Julia was suddenly worked up and indignant. "My head is my own house. Yes, that's it—the private house of my head." She'd remember that, because it was true. She was pleased at having thought of it.

Mrs. Redfern laughed. "Yes! If you can't be private inside your head, where can you be? I've thought of that at work. At least no one can see inside my head. That's mine, what's in there." Again she put her hand on Julia's knee, but this time gave it a pat.

Now they were coming into Shellmound Park. "Phee-ew-w-w!" burst out Julia. "Phew—phew—phew!" It was a ritual, just at this point, that had to be gone through as she always did.

"Quiet!" commanded Greg, not looking up.

"Greg," said Mrs. Redfern, "why must you read everywhere you go? It was touching when you were younger and Uncle Hugh called you the-little-boy-with-a-book, but now it gets very tiresome."

"Well, what do you want me to do?"

"Talk to us."

"O.K. What's the subject?" And he closed his book, but kept his place with his finger, Julia noticed, and looked at them, waiting.

"Greg, you're hopeless." Mrs. Redfern shook her head, but she had to smile.

"Yes, I know. Why can't you just accept it, Mother dear, and live with it." He settled back comfortably into his book again. Such a nice long journey to San Francisco and back by train and ferry. Most satisfactory, as he himself would say. "Better to be hopeless than ebullient like our Julia. Far less disturbing." If there was one thing Greg couldn't abide, it was being disturbed.

Julia chuckled. He was thirteen, but sometimes he talked like a professor and he did it on purpose to amuse himself. Ebullient. What did that mean? And she was about to ask when they drew to a stop under the vast dirty glass roof of the station, where you got off to board the ferry.

Julia ran ahead toward the wharf and, when she looked out, saw that the ferry was there waiting for them, dazzling white in the sunlight with its two gigantic black smokestacks. It was sitting in its slip between the pilings, columns of worn and scraped and splintered trunks of trees that had been rammed into the floor of the bay. Gulls sat in rows along the leveled-off tops preening their feathers. They would start up into the air for no apparent reason with a blurred winnowing of wings, then settle again a little way off and gaze out over the water as if watching for something.

Julia had her brown paper bag stuffed full of crusts that she and Mama and Greg had saved on the sly. If Gramma had known, she'd have had a fit over such wicked waste. "Perfectly good food for those great ugly birds!" She could have made a bread and butter pudding with those crusts. But Julia didn't think the seagulls were ugly, and it made her furious when Gramma said that. They were gray and snowy and smooth, and she could hardly wait (she never could) to go on board and for the starting signal to sound, that stomach-shattering bellow she could never get used to but that she waited for with shivers of happiness. And the gulls would fly up in a cloud, hovering over the boat from bow to stern, knowing what was in store.

Now here came Mama and Greg, while Julia hopped with impatience; then they pressed through the crowd along the broad plank that had been let down over the space between the wharf and the ferry where blackish-green water lolloped and slapped far below. She and Greg took their places at the rounded stern so that when the ferry turned and headed out across the bay they could watch its wake shaken out in a trail of white foam behind them while they flung up their crusts.

"I'll be inside—right in there," Mama said. "It's too glaring out here on deck. Here, Greg, give me your book." Off she went, and Julia never even looked round. She knew where Mama would be, always the same seat, and she always took Greg's book, but he usually got bored feeding the gulls before the last crust was gone.

Julia tossed and tossed until her arm ached, watching with delight how the birds swept in, their pink or greeny-yellow feet tucked up so neatly under their tails. They opened their beaks at precisely the right flick of a second, caught the crusts effortlessly with a turn of the head and a quick tilt of the body, then swept out again. And they all, every one of them, flew along one side of the boat up to the bow, were drawn as though by some invisible force along the other side back to the stern, then round they came again. She knew this because if there was a gull with a bad foot or one with special markings, she had noted him, and sure enough—round and round he went.

"Why?" she asked Greg. "Why do the gulls go round and round?"

He squinted his eyes against the sun to watch. "Yes, they do, don't they? I've never noticed. They fly forward to keep up and get their crusts as far as the bow, then let themselves be swept back in the slipstream on the other side as far as the stern, then fly forward again. That's very observing of you."

Julia was pleased. Slipstream. That's what she hadn't remembered, and what it did. Uncle Hugh had told her. Now their bag was empty and she watched the other children with envy. "Let's go up front, Greg, and see if the city's tottering."

Greg, leaning on the railing, idly noting whatever drifted past, shook his head in wonderment. "Child," he said, "are you still counting on an earthquake?"

"*Count*ing on it! What do you mean, *count*ing!" She was appalled.

"Of course you are. You know you are—a nice little one, just enough to shudder the Green Door around in midair and give you a tingle, but not to do any real damage."

"But it would be ghastly. I mean, Greg, what if it was just our luck to—"

"Ye gods. I'm going in. You're an abysmal nut, Julia, harping away about earthquakes. *You* go and look at the city. You might even get splashed."

What he meant was the time Julia, when she was six, had come home from her birthday lunch wearing a brand new hat that Mama had bought her in the city. As she stood on deck, suddenly everyone began looking at her and laughing until her face got scarlet. And she went in and told Mama, who gravely took off her hat and there, right on top, a gull had dropped a big white "do." She had never been so embarrassed.

She didn't know where to look and everyone in the seats around them was trying not to smile and poking each other about what had happened to that child's hat. Mama cleaned the "do" off with a piece of paper, then rolled the paper up into a ball and stuck it away somewhere. Julia wouldn't go out again for anything, but that was years and years ago and nothing like that had ever happened since.

Now she went up to the bow and stood there sternly watching the approaching city, studying the skyline, the tiny buildings, watching minutely to catch any slightest movement. Perhaps they must never go across again, she'd thought this morning. Never again take the chance.

But not go to the Green Door for her birthday? It was unthinkable.

She watched everything becoming clearer with an anxious heart—the Ferry Building with its clock tower and the warehouses along the bay front with taller buildings rising up behind. Yet excitement seethed in her at the thought of seeing Uncle Hugh again and opening her present from him and Aunt Alex, and seeing Hulda tonight, who would have baked her a birthday cake. She didn't know if she was more happy than scared, or more scared than happy. Somehow the two boiled up together and she drew in her breath suddenly and intensely, standing there with her hands gripping the railing.

2

Uncle Hugh's Earthquake

"Uncle Hugh! Uncle Hugh!" Julia saw him before Greg or Mama did. They'd gotten off the streetcar that went along Market and now, around the corner, there was the sign of the Green Door right near the flower seller's, and Uncle Hugh was waiting outside. He always got there first so as not to disappoint her and make her think he'd forgotten, and he had his package for her.

She raced toward him with her arms out, and he slipped the package under the branches of the potted palm that stood to one side of the entrance, caught her up and gave her a big hug the way he always did. Everything had to be the same, and of course it was, because what they did was natural for Uncle Hugh's kind of birthday celebration.

How handsome he was and how good he smelled—fresh, like clean wind. But then he'd driven here in his red runabout with the top down and this was what he would take them out to the park in, then home to his house for dinner that night.

"Happy birthday, Julia! What is it you are now? Nine, is it? Or ten? Oh, no—of course, twelve."

"Uncle *Hugh,* as if you didn't know—eleven!"

With his package under one arm and his other hand clasping hers, they all got into the little elevator, squashed in with two other people. The elevator swept up and stopped so suddenly it left Julia feeling gone inside. Now here was the green door and they went through it into a big airy room with enormous windows all the way around. San Francisco was laid out beneath, there was the blue bay beyond, and an almost invisible Oakland and Berkeley on the other side. It was a room full of conversation and laughter and the chink of silver, a room with green and gold wallpaper patterned over with scrolls of deep vermilion. There were ferns hanging from the ceiling, fresh flowers everywhere, and big, cushioned wicker chairs with high fan backs that made Julia feel like royalty.

Uncle Hugh had put his reservation in well ahead so as to get them a table at one of the windows, as he always did for Greg's and Mama's and their grandmother's birthday. He never failed them. He never failed them in anything, Mama had said once. Whereupon Julia, remembering, was aware of the faintest little twinge of sadness, yet knew not why, a twinge that immediately paled and was forgotten as the hostess led them to their table, seated them, and give them their menus.

But they weren't to choose yet. Julia had to open her

present, and they all watched while she undid the sumptuous ribbon Aunt Alex wrapped gifts in, and tore off the tissue—to reveal a large, thick book bound in dark green leather with her name stamped on the cover in gold down near the bottom and to the right. And when she opened it she found it was a book of blank pages, the first one hand-lettered in deep black, *The Private Journal of Julia Redfern*.

"Oh, but—Uncle *Hugh*—!"

There must have been some tone in her voice, for when she looked up she saw his face change. The light went right out of it. "Don't you like it, Julia? I had it made specially for you. Do you already have one?"

"Oh, no, no! And not *like* it—why, Uncle Hugh, it's the most—"

"Splendid," said Greg quietly.

"Yes, the most splendid present I have ever had. But Gram says my writing's a disgrace, and on top of that, how could I ever think up anything worthy enough to go in this book? What do *I* ever do? I'd have to be a queen—"

"But you're not to think up anything, Julia. Don't be self-conscious about it. It's not for grand happenings—I didn't give it to you for that. You're to put down whatever comes into your head. It won't matter what—"

"Whatever comes into my head. You mean secret, absolutely peculiar things I might not want to tell anybody because they wouldn't understand."

"Yes. Not that you went somewhere and came back and had a fight with Greg and went to bed. Not that sort of thing, all the old usual facts. But rags and tags of

oddities that you might lose forever if you never put them down."

"Julia does get rags and tags of oddities," murmured Celia Redfern.

Now the book was handed to Mama and then to Greg, and he smoothed his palm across the leather, opened it, turned it over, then reluctantly handed it back. Wouldn't he have loved it for his old Egyptians! Wouldn't he have loved to keep it; but his handwriting wasn't much better than hers.

Rags and tags of oddities. Yes, like the crack in the street she'd seen when they were walking out of the Ferry Building toward the streetcar. "Oh, *there*—!" and she'd stopped, stricken with shock and expectation for just an instant, waiting, poised, for the rumble to start, the crack to begin to widen, with other cracks springing away from it, their edges crumbling, and the dread grinding and crunching—"*Julia!*" cried out Mrs. Redfern. "Come on—come on!" and all the cars started honking, and she stared up and she was right in the midst of the traffic and Mama was darting back for her, grabbing her by the arm. "What is it, Julia? What's the matter—?"

She knew it would be no use trying to explain. Nobody would understand, not even Greg, because he would sensibly point out that the crack couldn't very well have got there (*if* it was an earthquake crack), couldn't even have begun without the rumbling and grinding and crunching coming first. Of course. But in that instant, catching sight of it right there in front of her, surely the biggest, widest one she'd ever seen in any street, she'd thought the earthquake was about to start. Maybe Uncle Hugh would understand. She'd try to tell him tonight. And yet, why? No, it was all very private, certainly something to go into the book he'd given her: exactly the way she'd felt in that awful split-second moment.

Julia got up suddenly and went around to him, leaned over and gave him a quick kiss on the cheek, then went back and sat down and didn't say anything. He seemed very pleased.

"Now, then," said the waitress, coming over, getting out her pad and pencil, and they all chose: Julia the Green Door chicken salad with their special dressing because she could have plenty of popovers to go with it, which she couldn't if she ordered a sandwich. But, Greg! He was impossible the way he always was, and took an endless time. "Interminable!" Mrs. Redfern said.

"But, Mom, this is a very serious business. Why should I choose anything I run even the slightest risk of getting at home?"

"How about lobster thermidor?" suggested the waitress at last.

Greg held up a long hand and looked at her rejectingly through his glasses. "Heaven forfend! A loathly mess, forsooth. I've seen it. Seafood is simply not to be considered."

The waitress's mouth quivered and she pressed her lips together. "Well, then, sir, how about the asparagus wrapped in ham with a nice tasty cheese sauce poured over?"

Julia snickered. Greg being called "sir"! "Come on, Cran, make up your mind. We're all perishing." The kids at school and those in the neighborhood called him Cran from when, at the age of eight, he'd suddenly become Professor Cranley (by his own naming) and took to giving information on whatever subject anybody needed to know about. And if he didn't know, he told them, he always knew where to look for it.

"Asparagus!" he said now in disgust. "Perish the thought. No, I'll have little thin pancakes with butter and powdered sugar and lingonberry jam."

"You mean and popovers, *too*, Greg?" exclaimed Mrs. Redfern. "*And* dessert?"

"Of course, my good woman. And why not? You know I have a stomach of iron." And it was true. He did.

Now Julia could settle into her happiness. You never really realized until afterwards, she'd found, just how happy you'd been compared to other times. But right at this moment she was sure she knew. She leaned down to put her precious book, wrapped in its tissue paper again, safely under her chair where nobody could step on it. Then she leaned forward with her elbows on the table and her chin on her palms.

"Now, Uncle Hugh, tell me about the time you were in the earthquake—and you shut up, Greg Redfern, and quit groaning. This is my birthday and if I want to talk about earthquakes, I can. Can't I, Mama? Or at least Uncle Hugh can."

"But, Julia," said Mrs. Redfern, "you've harped so lately. Couldn't we—just for now—?"

"No, I want to ask Uncle Hugh. What was it like? What *exactly* was it like when you were in the midst of it all?"

"But haven't I told you?"

"Oh, yes, once—sort of, but I've forgotten because it was ages ago, and now I want to know *exactly*. You were staying in a hotel—"

"Yes, on Geary, starting in on my first job over here, and just until I could decide where I wanted to live. About five in the morning—or, to be absolutely exact, Julia, at thirteen minutes after—I thought there must be a storm because I could hear thunder. Then there was a hideous sort of—wrench, and I realized the sound was coming up from underneath, a buried, vibrating thunder, deep and terrible. All at once I was trying to stand up, but that sickening rumbling and vibrating got worse and the furniture in my room started moving and the floor seemed to slide away from under my feet and I was thrown flat on my face.

"I struggled to get up, but I remember distinctly the feeling of not being able to, as if I were nailed to the floor so that I simply couldn't lift myself. As if I were held there by a magnet. And then an enormous wardrobe, a giant of a thing that must have weighed a ton, toppled over. I remember staring at the dusty top of it right in front of me and realizing that if I'd been thrown down a few feet farther along, my head would have been crushed by it.

"And all this time the building was being violently shaken and the thunderous roar kept up, and at the same time the crashing and smashing of falling masonry was going on and the scream of twisted and splintered wood. And somewhere, in the midst of it all, the insane jangling of a bell that I found out later was the tower bell of St.

Mary's Church in Chinatown, though of course all the church bells in the city must have been clashing together. I can't tell you what a nightmare—you can't begin to conceive. And then all at once the front of my room, a brick wall, simply crumpled away and fell into the street—the whole front of the hotel went down—and I stared around over my shoulder, because I was lying parallel to the street, and—" Uncle Hugh was gazing past Julia with widened eyes as if seeing the actual scene in front of him happening, just as she herself always did when she was in the deepest part of her making up, only Uncle Hugh was not making up. "I remember in just that instant, when the front wall fell away, seeing the building across the street sink straight down as if it were being swallowed whole in some giant chasm—"

"Yes—a huge crack opening, like the one I saw—"

"Only it wasn't a chasm. The building had simply fallen into rubble. And as I stared at the hole where it had been, I saw a little thin moon, serene and silvery, far off in the green sky. I'll never forget that, the look of that moon. And then the shaking stopped, and in those ten seconds of stillness between quakes, I managed to get into my pants and suit coat—dragged them on over my pajamas, though I don't remember doing it—and grasped the doorknob. But no matter how I twisted and shook it and pulled and wrenched, it was no use. The frame, the entire building had been twisted out of the straight so that the door was jammed and it was hopeless to try to get out. And just as I went across to the open front of the room to look down and judge if I could jump without being killed, and seeing the ruin in the street and knowing

19

I would be, the rumbling and shaking started up again. I managed to get over to the door somehow with the idea of breaking it down with my fists, and grabbed the knob —and it turned, because in just that second the door had become unjammed with the fresh bout of being shaken and twisted.

"I don't remember going along the hall. The next thing I knew I was on the stairs, being rattled and tossed down like a marble. And the stairs were swaying as if they were about to come loose in the next breath, splintered to matches, and bricks and glass were coming down everywhere. Then I was on the ground floor trying to get over a mass of rubble in my bare feet. Bricks were still falling, but though I found afterwards that my feet were cut and bleeding, I wasn't aware of any pain at the time. Then I was in the street running toward Market, and I saw water gushing up out of holes and I smelled gas—"

"Yes," said Julia. "That's it—the smell of gas."

"—and seeing streetcar tracks all twisted, and overhead wires coming down and whipping and wriggling along the ground and flashing blue sparks. And though the second quake was shorter than the first, it all seemed to go on forever. I didn't have the least idea where I was running to or why, nor did anyone else seem to, women in their nightgowns and men in pajamas, with their hair covered with plaster dust. It was like one of those awful dreams where you run and run and make no progress, as if you're pushing against time. But do you know how long it all lasted? Eighty seconds. The first quake was forty-five seconds, the stop in between ten, and the last twenty-five. But you count eighty seconds, Julia, and while you're doing it imagine you're in the midst of a city crashing around your ears—"

Julia closed her eyes and began counting, but just then the waitress came with the cart bearing their luncheon and began putting the plates around. And when she had everything in place and they could start, Mrs. Redfern said, "Now, Julia, you let Uncle Hugh—"

"Oh, but, Mama—then what happened, Uncle Hugh? *Then* what happened?"

He broke open a popover and buttered it while it was still beautifully hot, which was what they were all doing. No other restaurant had popovers, huge, delectable ones, like the Green Door. He took a bite of it, then went right on talking, managing to eat his lunch in the most casual, easy way without having to gulp and breathe in between mouthfuls the way Julia did when she was trying to tell something and eat at the same time.

"When the last quake stopped, it was the most uncanny thing, but you eat, now, Julia, or I won't say another word. When the last twenty-five seconds of shaking stopped, there wasn't a cry, not a sound from anyone. There was utter silence, and I remember the look on everyone's face. They were gray—hurt looking. I don't mean physically hurt, but as if they'd been horribly mistreated by someone they loved most, and couldn't bear it. As if they'd been deeply wronged and couldn't understand it. And they had been. The earth had stayed firm and quiet under their feet for all those years and they'd never thought much about it—then it had turned on them.

"While I was wandering around south toward the

hills, a tremendous explosion went off, because fires from overturned stoves in the wreckage all over the city had begun blazing up and one of them had set off the gasworks. Much later, when I got up high enough, I turned and looked out, and you can't imagine, Julia, what it's like to watch a city going up in flames. As I stood there, I saw two gigantic walls of fire racing toward each other, and I could hear fire engines clanging, and then the dynamiting began, to try to stop those two walls. There wasn't any water—the water mains had burst. And it was no use dynamiting, but it went on and on—fine big homes, still untouched, blown up to stop the fire that went on raging for three days and three nights."

"And what about Gramma and Mama—they didn't know what was happening to you all that time—"

"Not a word for the first day and night; then I got a ferry and went across to Berkeley."

"Did I ever tell you two about your grandmother?" said Mrs. Redfern. "We'd no idea what had happened to Uncle Hugh, and of course we were terribly worried about him. But your grandma looked over across the bay at that inferno lighting up the sky—I remember we could almost see to read by it at night—and she said, 'The hand of God, that's what it is. That wicked city—Sodom and Gomorrah!' And she actually believed that San Francisco was so wicked God had reached down and laid it low."

"And was it that wicked, Uncle Hugh?"

"Oh," said Uncle Hugh, cocking an eyebrow the way he would sometimes, and Mama too. They both did it. "Well, yes, you could say that it was a confoundedly wicked city—in spots. What did people do? Well, down on the Barbary Coast were the Chinese quarters, and all kinds of characters went there to gamble and smoke opium, and people were strangled and knifed and robbed in back alleys. Oh, it was bad all right. And all the time this was going on, my friend Willie Templeton and I were having a marvelous time in other parts of the city. Did I ever tell you it was because of the fire I met Aunt Alex?"

He leaned back in his chair, smiling to himself, and when their waitress came near, held out his hand in the most elegant way she had ever seen, Julia thought, and beckoned to her.

"Well, Julia, and are you going to manage dessert as well? No, of course not. I can't imagine Julia could possibly want anything more. So that's settled. Now, let's see—as for the rest of us—" and he took the menu and glanced it over with a cool, considering expression, never even looking at her.

"Uncle *Hugh!*" Of course he was teasing her. He loved to tease, and he knew perfectly well she always had strawberry tart with whipped cream on top. It was as much a part of her birthday as Hulda's incomparable cake would be tonight, of which there would be half left to take home so that Gramma could have some and they could finish it off, the four of them.

And when the waitress had cleared their plates away and gone for their tarts, "No, I didn't know how you met Aunt Alex."

"Well, I finally found Willie Templeton in one of the tents that had been set up in the park. Alex and her family were nearby, and when I first looked at her—she was only seventeen at the time—I thought she was the most beautiful thing I'd ever seen."

"She wasn't fat in those days, I guess," said Julia, seeing Aunt Alex in her mind as she was now, large, slow, regal, and infinitely comfort loving, with a bosom upon which necklaces lay on a vast slope, then "plunged over the precipice," Julia always said, "and swung."

Mama put her hand over her face, then looked at Uncle Hugh.

"Honestly, Jule," said Greg, and flicked his glasses into place.

"Well, what have I said? *Isn't* Aunt Alex fat?"

"You don't *say* 'fat,' you say 'stout.'"

Uncle Hugh chuckled. "You wouldn't have known Aunt Alex in those days, though of course she's still beautiful, isn't she? She had dozens of beaus, some very well-off like her own people, and why she ever picked me I cannot imagine. I've often thought what a bad bargain she made."

Julia stared at him in astonishment. "Why, what do you mean, a bad bargain! She's the luckiest woman in the world and she knows it—"

"Don't be absurd, Hugh," said Mama quietly. "I agree with Julia." Of course she agreed. Of all her brothers, Uncle Hugh was her favorite. Julia didn't even know the others—scattered across the world, and Uncle Artie dead, killed in the war like Julia's father.

"Oh, no," said Uncle Hugh, and there was that strange little look at the corners of his eyes that Julia had seen before and could never understand, as if the skin had gotten tight, and there was a certain expression around his mouth. "No talent, no money. She could have done a million times better."

"I don't believe it," said Julia passionately. "You're handsome, and you *do* have m—"

"That's all right," and Mama reached her hand over to press Julia's in a way Julia knew. It meant definitely, "Say no more." And the tarts came—Uncle Hugh, apparently, wasn't having one—and Mama went on talking about something else while Julia sat there eating hers and looking at him, wondering why that queer little twinge of sadness had come back that she had felt before. When was it? Yes, when they were crossing to their table and she'd remembered Mama saying Uncle Hugh never failed them. But why would that make anybody sad? And then, now, here it was again, that twinge of sadness, maybe because Uncle Hugh had the funny tight look at the outer corner of his eyes and around his mouth.

Once Uncle Hugh at dinner had cracked his favorite little joke about London in a fog when trains become dew and are mist, and Aunt Alex rapped out in sharp irritation, "Oh, Hugh, you and your puns. Do you have to play the same old record again and again?" And Julia had blazed up at her because Aunt Alex had never appreciated Uncle Hugh—never—and was always calling him for something, bossing him, keeping at him in her mostly ladylike way, very smooth and even-handed, pretending she was teasing, but sometimes like this, quite open and rude and hurtful.

"You must not have any sense of humor," burst out Julia, "or you wouldn't say a thing like that. Greg and I love Uncle Hugh's puns!"

Aunt Alex gave Julia a cool and level look and Uncle Hugh was silent, then tried to pass it off, and Mama sent Julia away from the table and told her afterwards that she must never again enter into a difference between Aunt Alex and Uncle Hugh, because it only made everything more difficult. *Did* Julia promise? No, she did not, and sat there seething in Uncle Hugh's study, though after a while she gave in, but only for Uncle Hugh's sake. Mama said that Uncle Hugh "understood" Aunt Alex and that most of the time she really was only teasing.

But why did he have to go and marry a woman like that? And what had he meant, "no talent, no money," when he was head of a bank (Julia wasn't exactly sure about that) and must be awfully rich. He'd have to be to have a house like his, and to afford the way Aunt Alex dressed and the places they went. Julia didn't understand.

But she understood one thing: why he wasn't having a strawberry tart with whipped cream on top, and he'd had only one popover. He didn't want to get fat like Aunt Alex.

3

The Toppling Pine

It was positively hot in the sun, at least for San Francisco. Above the park, the sky hadn't a cloud. Uncle Hugh and Mama were settled under a tree beyond earshot of the band while Greg, in the museum, mooned around the Egyptian section over the mummies and artifacts.

Julia raced toward the top of the slope, then stood poised, deciding on that single pine down there as her goal. Before her, under the brilliance, stretched acres of grass—surely acres, for that dark line of trees on the far side seemed miles away. This was the lawn of her castle, and in the trees where she'd been exploring were statues, all mossy, that had been there for centuries, as long as her family had owned this place. Several figures wended their way slowly across, mother and father with picnic basket and coats and blankets, and two children shouting at each other, straggling behind. Villagers, of course, come to leave their peelings and apple cores and papers scattered over the grounds. She'd have to tell her gardeners to put up those signs again, "Keep out! This means *You!*"

Filled with an indescribable ecstasy she started down. She ran—she ran, faster, faster. And suddenly the world spun and something glinted. Her shoes had slipped and she went headlong, shouting for joy, rolling, like Jennie, Uncle Hugh's collie, let out for a romp, over and over, until she landed at the pine, cheek pressed into the thick, delicious-smelling grass. And her eyes widened with shock.

A rumbling, a kind of deep reverberating thud, sounded in her ear. She turned over and stared up, mouth aghast, breath stopped, and the pine wheeled backward over her head, tilted toward earth. She squeezed her eyes shut, looked again, and there it was, wheeling and tilting, sickeningly rolling down the sky, and she sprang up and staggered away, stumbling and crying out for Uncle Hugh. "Uncle Hugh—Uncle Hugh—!" and got up the slope somehow, crawling on her hands and knees, then up again, running, panting with terror—and with something else as well. Something else. "Uncle Hugh, it's the—"

At the top she had to catch her breath. But how strange—because Uncle Hugh and Mama hadn't moved. Uncle Hugh had his knees up with his arms clasped around them, and now he flung out a hand and made a circle to go with whatever he was saying, and Mama was on her side, lying down, with one elbow propping up the top part of her while she listened to what Uncle Hugh

28

was telling, and other people were walking around over there behind them, quite calmly. No one was running. No one was desperate. The museum had not crumbled into ruin.

Julia turned and stared at the pine. It was upright, its boughs swaying in the rising wind that was bringing in the first long drifts of fog from the sea. She got down and applied an ear to the ground. There it was again— that deep reverberation, with every now and then a series of thuds. She looked off across the park and thought. She had seen the pine sway and fall toward her. Twice she'd looked, two separate times. And it had swayed and horribly tilted.

She got up and walked over to Uncle Hugh and Mama, and it seemed they must have been speaking of something they didn't want her to know about, because they stopped when they saw her coming. She had a kind of feeling.

"*What?*" she said.

"Nothing, Julia," said Mama. "Why don't you go in and find Greg, and we'll be along soon. It's getting cold— the fog's coming in." Julia looked at them, but nothing in their faces gave the secret away. If they had a secret. "Go on now. It'll take you forever to get to the museum the way you wander around, and then you'll want to look for a bit. We'll be there."

In front of the museum, families were still sitting on rows of folding chairs under the curious little trees that had their tops all sheared off flat and the band was still pumping away, with crashes of those big polished brass

plates every now and then and the peal of trumpets streaming through the pomp of sound.

Julia serenely lost herself in the museum rooms as she always did—perfect, with no one to urge her on, call her back, take her by the arm, come and collect her when she didn't want to be collected—and finally arrived in the Egyptian Room, where Greg, solitary, brooded over a case. What did he think about? What did he see? Just the jewels and mirrors and boxes and combs and ornaments and figurines that had been fashioned five thousand years ago?

She went to him and he raised his head, and she might have been a stranger, and not a welcome one.

"Hail, Your Stuffiness, it's time to go. Uncle Hugh and Mama'll be along any minute." He paid no attention; he went on examining. "Greg," she said presently, "something peculiar."

"What?" he said, not looking up. She told him exactly how everything had happened, first one thing and then another, and how she had thought it was the beginning of an earthquake. She couldn't understand. She had heard the deep rumbling in the earth when she'd listened again, a rumbling and thudding, but when she turned and looked back, the pine was still standing, just as it always had.

Greg raised up and studied her, as though deeply considering. He loved this sort of thing: being given the facts, laying them all out, tracking down the explanation.

"Well, now," he said finally, like a lawyer attacking a problem. "You fell, you said, then rolled down the entire slope. Correct?"

"Yes," said Julia. "Correct," she added, so that he would go on, because there was a certain way of doing all this.

"Then a second or two later, after listening to the thud in the ground, you looked up at the pine. It seemed to sway. Naturally, because you were dizzy. If you had rolled from left to right down the slope, I have an idea the tree would have swayed one way. If from right to left, another. Not sure. Make a note: try this at home." Julia pretended to make a note, and Greg continued. "Very well," and here he paused and studied the floor gravely, and Julia didn't giggle because she knew perfectly well he was being either Professor Cranley or Sherlock Holmes, and she was his secretary. "With reference to the thumping, or thudding, this, I believe, was the band, or more likely the bass drum, transmitting its thuds and thumps through the earth."

"What's 'transmitting'?" said Julia. "What's that?"

"Sending. You can always hear something at a distance through the earth more distinctly than you can through the air. Not sure why. Make a note: look up transmission through earth. Now, then, next. The rumbling. That rumbling was the traffic out on the avenue behind the museum. It may not have been, but I'll bet it was because there's nothing else that would have made a rumble coming through the earth. A continuous rumble, was it?"

"Yes. Continuous. Going on and on, if that's what you mean."

"That's it. So there's your problem solved. And there

wasn't any earthquake, much as you excruciatingly wanted one, and hoped for it. All clear?"

Julia considered him, then turned away, dragging a finger along the top of the case. She *was* an abysmal nut. It was so obvious, why hadn't she thought of it? But then she didn't know about transmission and things like that. And then she'd been too frightened. Also, she *had* been wanting—no, no—why had Greg said that? Expecting something to happen. But—hoping for it, wanting it? Yes. Hadn't there been that other feeling along with her terror? What she'd felt on the boat, looking across the water at the skyline of the city? Listening to Uncle Hugh? An almost trembling excitement? But why, when everything is so frightful in an earthquake? How *could* she have hoped for it? It was all so mixing, to feel two things at once, as if she were two different persons.

Now there came an echoing, and voices, and here were Mama and Uncle Hugh.

"Greg," said Mrs. Redfern, "don't you ever get sick of your old mummies?"

Julia turned to look at him, saw a slight, mysterious smile around his mouth, and there was a light in his eyes behind his glasses; his narrow face, too, with its beaky nose, seemed alight.

"I've made a decision," he said finally. "I'm going to write my own history of the Egyptians with all my own illustrations, in pen and ink and watercolor. The whole thing written my own way." Now his glance went beyond Mama as if seeing it, just exactly as it would be. And Julia, because she knew Greg so well, knew that *he* was excited—maybe even more than she'd been about her earthquake. Well, excited differently because it was important to him. "Strange I've never thought of doing it before."

"But, Greg," said Mrs. Redfern, "aren't there already dozens of histories?"

The look in his large, almond-shaped eyes seemed to put her at a distance. "What's that got to do with anything?" he said. "I'm going to write Greg Redfern's."

4

When Jennie Danced

Aunt Alex surged toward them across the polished floor laid with a Persian rug. Her little heels clicked, then were silenced. On the long hall table a vase at least two feet high held a mass of large mixed flowers, lavish, fragrant, their colors reflected in the mirror behind. In the gray and gold living room Hulda had lighted a fire, and in there, too, flowers sent fragrance from tables, from the top of the Steinway, from the marble mantle. Inside this house, in the high-ceilinged hall with the curved stairway leading up, all was warm and inviting. Outside, fog pressed against the windows from which, on clear days, you looked down over San Francisco and the bay to the east and the Golden Gate to the north. "A-a-a-ah, *uh!*" went the foghorn in the channel. "A-a-a-ah, *uh!*" like a wounded bull. But the call was fainter now that they'd come in. Everything in this big house was quiet, subdued, muffled. You never heard the traffic.

Aunt Alex bent, allowed her smooth cheek to be kissed, and murmured in Julia's ear, "Happy birthday, dear. Happy birthday!" But even as Julia was saying, "Thank you, Aunt Alex. And thank you for the beautiful—" Aunt Alex was already turning away to throw her arms around Greg, having this at least in common with Gramma: she adored Greg. She was fatuous about him.

"And here's my Greg, taller than ever. I think he's going to be over six feet, don't you, Celia? A fine, tall, handsome young man."

"With glasses?" said Julia.

"Of course with glasses," said Aunt Alex indignantly. "What have glasses to do with it? He'll be distinguished looking. Very distinguished. A professor, of course."

"Not a professor, Alex," said Mama. "An Egyptologist."

"Oh, well—one and the same thing, surely," said Aunt Alex, waving her hand, then all at once gave Uncle Hugh a quick, questioning look.

"Where's Jennie?" demanded Julia all at once. Why hadn't Jennie come dashing to meet them, springing up to put her paws on Julia's shoulders so that she could give her a lick, letting out little yelps of joy, panting, prancing on her hind legs, her feathery tail lashing from side to side? Julia tore off her coat, threw it onto a chair, and ran out to the kitchen.

"*Hulda—!*" and she grabbed Hulda around her middle and tried to dance her across the room. And Hulda, scarcely taller than Julia, red-faced, bright blue-eyed, with her straw-colored graying hair done in a coronet around her head, let out a gasp.

"Oh!" she said, holding up her floury hands from making the biscuits. "Oh, Julia—Julia!" and wouldn't tell where the cake was, no matter how Julia teased, but the teasing was all part of the fun. "No, no," cried Hulda, laughing. "Oh, what a bear—a regular bear you are with your hugs. You'll be too big for me one of these days—too big entirely."

Suddenly Julia quieted and looked around. She went to the door into the garden and opened it and looked out. No Jennie. When she turned to Hulda, Hulda had commenced rolling out the dough for the biscuits on the big clean kitchen table. "But, Hulda, where's Jennie?"

Hulda stared up. She seemed shocked. "You mean they didn't tell you?" Julia could give no answer, there was such a terrible feeling in her stomach. "She had to go to the vet's, dearie."

"What do you mean, she had to go? What was the matter? When will she be back?"

"Oh, Julia. They should have told you. Jennie was sick—very sick. She died about a week ago." Then Hulda's eyes widened and she smacked her hand across her mouth. "Oh, Lord, maybe I shouldn't have said—"

Julia could feel her face getting scarlet. A week ago— a whole week. And Uncle Hugh hadn't said a word, not one single word, because he hadn't wanted to spoil her birthday. And yet it had to be spoiled some time. But spoiled—*spoiled*. She would never see Jennie again. Imagine calling *that* spoiling a birthday! She could feel her mouth going into the awful shape she knew so well,

and her throat tightening so that she could scarcely breathe.

She opened the door into the garden, closed it behind her, and raced down the brick path that led through the formal beds of roses, right down to the end where there was an arbor and she could go inside and nobody could see her. Now the tears welled up and spilled over and she let out a wail of grief that came up out of the pit of her paining stomach, then sat down and sobbed until she'd got over the worst part. She wiped her face on her skirt, sat there thinking about Jennie, wept again, and finally got up and went out into the garden. Greg was sitting on a bench outside the dining room windows, his head down, and he was doing something with a coin, turning it and turning it between his fingers the way he could do.

She went to him and sat beside him. "Do you know, Greg? Did they tell you?" He nodded. "Did you love Jennie?"

"Well, of course," he said abruptly. He sounded angry, stifled.

"But you said after Smokey got run over that you'd never love another cat—or any other animal. Like, but not love."

"Well, you can't just *plan* everything."

"Maybe Uncle Hugh'll get another collie."

"I'll bet he won't. Jennie was special—and he's had her since she was a puppy. I don't know if he'd want another dog. *I* wouldn't," said Greg with such passion that Julia stared at him in astonishment. Greg didn't often get worked up over things. He couldn't bear people getting into states, only Julia, because she was just a kid and such an abysmal nut anyway, you expected it of her. But grown-ups, and himself, that was different. When Gramma and Mama got irked at each other, and raised their voices, he'd go out of the room, and he couldn't stand it if Mama got after him. He was stubborn, just as stubborn as Julia, but he'd never answer back, just go away with everything bottled up inside of him. He would never argue. But that didn't mean he'd changed his mind or given in.

Now Uncle Hugh appeared at one of the long dining room windows and opened it. "Come in, you two," he said quietly. "It's time for dinner. Hulda's all ready." There was a little silence and he came out and put his hand on Julia's head and smoothed her hair back. "I'm sorry, Julia. So very sorry I couldn't tell you. But I wanted your birthday to be perfect as long as it could be. Perhaps I did things the wrong way—I often do."

Hearing Uncle Hugh speak like that, in a particular voice, Julia felt the treacherous tears bulging up again, and she got up and butted her head against his chest, then went inside, quickly, and down the hall to the bathroom where she bathed her face in cold water to get the tear streaks off and to cool her cheeks. She wasn't going to go out and sit at the table in front of Aunt Alex at her own birthday dinner looking a wreck and a mess. She even combed through her wild reddish brown mop with Aunt Alex's jeweled comb, which lay, together with its companion brush, at a certain angle on the spotless starched linen mat. Aunt Alex's bathrooms, Julia always thought, were such wonders to behold in all their shining beauty that it almost seemed sacrilegious to sit on the toilets.

Perhaps it was because of Jennie they let her talk, or because it was her birthday. Usually Mama said, "Well, I think that'll do for now, Julia," but not, for some reason, this evening. She was telling them about the brown bungalow they'd lived in, Mama and Greg and Julia and their father, before he'd been killed in the war, and for a little while afterwards. Then Mrs. Weed, that scraggy woman, their landlady, who'd looked to Julia just like a weed, had gone and sold it right out from under them, and after all the work Mama and Daddy had put into it, painting every single room and cleaning and polishing the paneling in the living room, and scraping the bricks of the fireplace. But of course, it was *because* they'd fixed it all up that she'd sold it. But that wasn't what Julia was talking about.

She'd gone by there the other day, she was saying, and what do you think? In that beautiful front garden, where Julia and Maisie used to play behind the blackberry vines and eat blackberries hot from the sun, they'd put up a big, ugly old stucco apartment building. And now the brown bungalow had its face, without any garden at all, smashed right up against the back of the apartment house, with all the old scrub mops and floor rags and garbage pails only a few feet from the bungalow's front door. "It made me sick. I almost cried. A hideous big yellow building trimmed in dog-do brown—"

41

"Julia!" said Mama. "Khaki, you mean."

"No, I do not mean khaki. A regular sightsore, that's what it is—and not a tree left."

"Oh, Julia!" said Aunt Alex. "You're marvelous. Never could anyone purposely think up anything like that— sightsore." Aunt Alex never spared her on these occasions when she thought Julia had make a mistake, just laughed and laughed and said Julia was the limit.

"It's 'eyesore,' Jule," said Greg. "Not 'sightsore.'"

"*Eye*sore! I don't believe it. That's a horrible word— eyesore. Positively repuganant. My eyes weren't sore. The *sight* was sore. I'm going to go look it up, and I'll bet anything you're wrong." She always bet Greg anything he was wrong, but she hadn't won yet. And sure enough—no "sightsore," but "eyesore," yes, and it meant exactly what she'd had in mind: something unpleasant to look at. Oh, golly. It was embarrassing, as usual, but she would never learn—not to be so sure about things, she meant. But she always *was* sure; she couldn't help herself. Now she'd have to stick here, in Uncle Hugh's study, looking up words until Hulda had cleared away and brought in the cake, so that in among the compliments to Hulda about it, she could slip in and no one would pay any attention.

She heard Hulda, and then Aunt Alex's exclamations.

"Do you know, Celia," Aunt Alex was saying to Mama as Julia came back along the hall, "do you know that one of my closest friends—or so I thought—tried to get Hulda away from me? Can you imagine that, such treachery? Why, I'd rather give up Hugh than Hulda!" She was laughing as she said it, or rather laughed right after she said it—that last sentence—and looked down the table at Uncle Hugh, Julia saw as she came in, then glanced up and took in Julia's expression. "Oh, I'm teasing, child—teasing!"

Yes, but I bet you *would* rather give up Uncle Hugh than Hulda. Julia slid into her chair, gazing at the cake, which Hulda had put at her place so that she could blow out the candles. Julia reached around and squeezed Hulda's bony, bright-red hand—it was an angel food, Hulda said, with three layers. It had thick, silky-smooth, pale yellow icing with frosted flowers and leaves, the flowers strewn across the top and down the sides, and there were sprays of jasmine all around the base.

Julia wished, drawing in her breath and slowly letting it out the way Uncle Hugh had told her to do so as to get every last one of the eleven candles. Then Hulda took the cake round to Aunt Alex so that it could be neatly cut (*not* the way Julia would have done it) and probably so that Aunt Alex could be sure of getting a nice large slice, popped into Julia's head. How Aunt Alex loved desserts, Hulda's cakes, her pies with their melting pastry, *bombes glacés* ("Make glassy bombs, Hulda," Julia would beg), baked Alaskas, meringues with ice cream inside and sugared berries dripped all over, and chocolate mousse, which Julia thought must be chocolate mouse when she'd first heard Aunt Alex ask for it.

Now Hulda came around to each place with ice cream for the cake, ice cream Hulda herself had made, patiently turning and turning the handle of the bucket with the ice in the bottom of it until the cream went firm. Naturally there was none more delectable, certainly not that you could buy.

"Do you know what I wished, Uncle Hugh?"

"Don't tell me, Julia, it won't come true."

"Oh, yes, it will. I wished with all my might that you'd find another—" Another puppy, just like Jennie when she was little, she'd been going to say, but never got it out, hesitating just before "puppy," because perhaps she shouldn't tell after all, and in that small silence something happened that Julia never forgot.

All at once, from out there in the kitchen, came the sound of Jennie's claws dancing on the linoleum the way she always danced when Hulda was about to feed her. "Dance, Jennie!" Hulda would say. "Come and dance for me, my beauty." And Jennie would dance, her claws clicking, and let out a single yelp of excitement. And Julia always swore afterwards that she had heard Jennie's quick little yelp, just one.

She looked around the table. Aunt Alex was staring at Uncle Hugh in aghast disbelief, and so was Mama, and Greg; then Greg looked over at her, but Mama and Aunt Alex were still frozen as they had been, with their eyes fixed on Uncle Hugh, Aunt Alex with her mouth slightly open as if she'd forgotten to close it. Then slowly—slowly —Uncle Hugh pushed back his chair and went out, leaving the dining room door open behind him. They heard him say something to Hulda from beyond the butler's pantry, questioning her about Jennie, then Hulda's answer,

"No, Mr. Penfield, not a sound."

Presently Uncle Hugh came back, the queerest expression on his face, and without a word sat down and rested his forehead on his hand. Then he looked up.

"But you heard her, of course, Alex? Celia?"

Mama didn't answer, and Aunt Alex, who was now calmly continuing to eat her cake and ice cream, glanced up as if in surprise. "What do you mean, Hugh?"

"Well, you know perfectly well what I mean," he burst out incredulously. "Jennie! Jennie dancing in the kitchen! You heard her, Celia!"

"Yes, Hugh, I did—"

"And *I* did, Aunt Alex," shouted Julia, "*I* did. And so did you. I saw the way you were looking at Uncle Hugh, with your mouth open as if you couldn't believe it." How *could* Aunt Alex sit there with that casual, faintly surprised look on her face, and say "What do you mean?" How *could* she! "And you did, too, didn't you, Greg?"

He hesitated before answering. "I certainly thought I heard something."

"So there, Aunt Alex."

"Nonsense," said Aunt Alex sharply. "Utter nonsense. Jennie is dead. She is buried. There is no way on earth we could have heard Jennie's claws clicking on the linoleum. Not with the door closed."

"But it wasn't," said Uncle Hugh. "Hulda was in the pantry and had left the door open. Not that such a thing as doors open or closed matter in the least under these circumstances. And you are saying 'clicking,' which means you heard her. That was exactly what we heard, and *you* did, or you wouldn't have used that word."

45

"Oh, Hugh, let's not be medieval!" flung out Aunt Alex. "I heard nothing. Jennie always made clicks when she danced. And you said you heard her dancing. You said it, I didn't. And *if* you heard her, that's *what* you would have heard."

Aunt Alex's two favorite words were "bizarre" and "medieval," the first "e" in "medieval" pronounced as in "led." She would use it in discussions about anything not to be explained. And as for her other word, she would say of someone, some new acquaintance, "She is positively the most bizarre creature I have ever met," meaning that she looked or acted or dressed or spoke in a way Aunt Alex thought ridiculous or didn't approve of.

"Then why did you look at me as you did?" demanded Uncle Hugh. "You looked exactly as if you were hearing what the rest of us heard."

"Because I couldn't understand for the life of me what had struck you!"

"Well, I'm not being medieval, as you put it." Uncle Hugh looked at Mama, and she returned him her assenting look, their eyes meeting in the old conspiracy of brother and sister who understood one another.

"I only know," said Aunt Alex, "that no random sounds, which Hulda didn't hear, are going to make a fool of me. I don't, and will not believe in the impossible, the supernatural."

Which meant that the rest of them *were* fools, and as Aunt Alex, according to her often-repeated statement, did not suffer fools gladly, this always put her comfortably on the other side of the fence, Grandma pointed out. "And there're a goodly number across from her as

46

far as Alex is concerned, you can bet your boots on that."

"What do *you* think, Hugh?" asked Mama.

"I don't know—if you mean how did it happen. But I do say that anything is possible, and that simply because we don't understand, we have no right to say that it didn't happen. Would you agree, Greg?"

Sitting over there between Aunt Alex at one end, who expected him always to take her side, and Uncle Hugh at the other, who expected his honest opinion, Greg nodded. "Right-o, Uncle Hugh, right-o."

Aunt Alex tossed her head. "*Well*," she said, "are we through here? Let's go into the other room and talk about something else. I've had quite enough of this absurd conversation."

5

The Truth About Uncle Hugh

Aunt Alex, having buttonholed Greg thoroughly about
his studies (she always called them that, as though he
were already in college), went up to bed early. She had a
headache, she said. But Julia thought perhaps it was because she could feel the rest of them wanting to talk
about Jennie and about different incidents in the Penfield family, Mama's and Uncle Hugh's, cases of second
sight, premonitions, appearances, and other extraordinary
happenings.

For instance, there was the time Mama and Uncle
Hugh reminded each other of, that time right after
Grandpa died. (Now they were all sitting around the fire,
Greg and Mama on the couch, Uncle Hugh in his leather
chair with his feet up, and Julia cross-legged on the floor
opposite him, all of them peaceful and in accord. Aunt
Alex, upstairs, would be reading a detective novel in

bed and drinking coffee, everybody knew, which in com-
bination was one of her special pleasures. Julia had often
imagined her slipping off her corsets—"U-uph, what a
relief!" especially after a big dinner—getting into her
tentlike nightgown, all lace and ribbon, climbing into
that vast softness, and settling herself among her pillows.
Pure heaven.)

Mama and Uncle Hugh and Gramma, it seemed, were
sitting together talking on the evening after the funeral
when they heard Grandpa's familiar footsteps coming
along the veranda. They had raised their heads, expecting the doorbell to ring and wondering who it could possibly be, walking like that—and then, "rap, rap, ratta-tat-
tat—rap, rap," exactly the way Grandpa always did when
he arrived home with his arms full of groceries and
wanted Gramma to come and open the door so he
wouldn't have to get out his key, or he'd do it sometimes
on one of the veranda windows just to let them know he
was there. Uncle Hugh had gotten up immediately and
opened the door—went right along the veranda and out
into the garden, and there wasn't a soul—not a soul anywhere. The street was empty.

Greg, apparently, had heard this story. "But you
never told *me*!" exclaimed Julia. "You never told *me* that
one!" She was highly indignant. She was supposed to
know all the family stories; she expected to. How could
they have left that one out!

"Oh, didn't we?" said Mama. "And then there was the
time, during the war, when I woke early in the morning
and saw Artie standing at the foot of the bed." Artie had
been the youngest brother, younger than Mama. "I

looked at him and sat up and said 'Artie!' and he smiled at me and nodded, then faded from sight. After a moment or two I got up and went to the window and drew back the curtains. I absolutely had not been asleep when I saw him, and I knew he'd been killed. Sure enough, your grandma got the telegram a day or two later."

Nobody said anything. Then, "But you never saw Dad after he was killed, did you, Mama?"

"No, Julia, never your father."

Julia lay in the big guest room bed beside Mama, listening to the foghorn and thinking. The light had been turned out an hour or more ago, but she and Mama had been talking. "Why do you s'pose Aunt Alex told that fib about not hearing Jennie?"

"Does it occur to you, Julia, that possibly Aunt Alex was telling the truth? She said she looked surprised because of the look on our faces—on Uncle Hugh's, and she couldn't figure it out. That was quite possible."

"No," said Julia. "I saw her. I was looking at her when it happened, and she heard Jennie at exactly the very second we did."

Mama gave a little laugh. "How like your grandmother you are. You say she never, never sees your side, and always finds fault with you but never with Greg. And you're just that way with Aunt Alex. You never see her side, and always find fault with her, but never with Uncle Hugh. I can't imagine Uncle Hugh doing one thing that would make you see it as a fault. He's right, he's perfect, and Aunt Alex is always wrong."

Julia pondered this notion. "Well," she said finally, "Aunt Alex did so hear Jennie."

Mama turned over, facing away toward the windows which meant she wanted to go to sleep and that Julia was to keep quiet. But something had started because of what Mama had said about Uncle Hugh: that he couldn't do one thing that Julia would ever see as a fault. And it had to do—her thoughts starting up—with their going home in the morning, back to that stuffy little house in Berkeley she and Gramma and Greg and Mama lived in. Gramma's house. Gramma had the biggest bedroom, which wasn't very big, and Mama and Julia had the other, which was tiny, and Greg slept on a pull-out couch in the living room. It was after their father had been killed in the war, and they had had to move out of the brown bungalow because of its being sold, that for some reason they moved in with Gramma.

It was true Julia was always getting into a fix with her, but she always *did* find fault with Julia but hardly ever with Greg. Julia banged doors, let in flies, left her things around in a mess, "oozed" when she was full of rebellion, so that "the whole house," Gramma said, "reeked of Julia." No matter what went wrong, "Ju-*lia!*" Gramma would explode, with that awful, furious, upward twitch on the last part of her name. Or "*Ju*lia!" when she refused to answer because it probably wasn't her fault, or if it was, she'd get a going-over for it. The minute Mama got home from work, she got the whole story in detail from Gramma.

The thing was, thought Julia, *why* did they have to

go on living with her? She'd got the idea from Greg. He'd had his drawings and charts spread all over the dining room table for a special project that called for extremely touchy pen-and-ink work. And right in the middle of it he had to put everything away in boxes under Gramma's bed because people were coming, and there wasn't anyplace else to put them. He was always having to do this; he had no place at all to keep his belongings. But on that day Julia heard him say to Mama, with an edge to his voice that came when he was too bottled up, "What a relief if only Uncle Hugh could get us a house the way he did Grandma—" They had stuck in Julia's mind, those words of Greg's, because he so seldom let out his deepest, most private feelings.

Julia couldn't remember what her mother said, or if she said anything, but why *did* Uncle Hugh let them go on living with Gramma when he knew perfectly well how squeezed they were? And she felt a pain gathering in her stomach, first because she was finding fault with Uncle Hugh. Compared to this house, Gramma's would fit into two rooms of it. Just for fun, Greg had figured it out. Second, because of having to go home from the spaciousness and fragrance of this big house to that other quite often smelly little one. Gramma would cook tripe and onions, or liver and onions (Julia hated them both), or serve soup with a big bald boiled potato sitting in the middle of it. Or she would fix up bubble-and-squeak out of old brussels sprouts and bits of left-over meat and gravy with second-day mashed potatoes on top, and the brussels sprouts sent their powerful aroma all over the house.

"Julia, what on earth is the matter, dear? Why are you flopping around like that? How do you expect me to go to sleep—I've got so much to do when we get home. Now be still." Julia tried but she was taken with the fidgets. "Oh, darling, what *is* it? Have you got a stomach-ache? Did you eat too much?"

Julia couldn't answer. All was silent, and then, "A-a-a-ah, *uh!*" went the foghorn. "A-a-a-ah, *uh!*" She stared up into the darkness and the pain was still there in her stomach when finally she fell asleep.

Hulda had given Julia a big paper bag full of crusts for the gulls and now they were almost gone.

"Greg, isn't Uncle Hugh terribly rich?"

"Not Uncle Hugh. Didn't you know? Aunt Alex."

Julia was stunned. "You mean he isn't at *all*?"

"Well, he's head of some department at the bank, but that's nothing compared to what Aunt Alex has. What he makes, I mean."

"How do you know?"

"Because of what Grandma's said."

But she, Julia, had never heard anything like that. She'd never heard Gramma say a thing about Uncle Hugh's money. Why did she seem to miss so much that Greg knew about?

"Why is Aunt Alex rich and Uncle Hugh isn't?"

"Because she inherited a whole pile from her family and Grandma says she bets anything Aunt Alex keeps a finger on every penny."

Julia had ceased throwing crusts while she absorbed all this astounding information piece by piece, turned it over in her mind and painfully reshaped first one idea and then another of those she'd held about Uncle Hugh. And the sea gulls floated by, their heads turned toward her, their yellow eyes watching while she stood at the rail, her hand poised inside the bag. It was something— this that Greg had told her—she would never have guessed, never could possibly have guessed. But now she understood. No wonder Aunt Alex was so bossy with Uncle Hugh; and without having to explain anything to herself, answers to scene after scene, most that she didn't even have to call to mind, fell into place.

Now all at once she thought of something else because of talking about Uncle Hugh. "Why, Greg? Why did we have to move in with Gram?"

"Because Dad owed money and it's had to be paid back. It still is. He never made much trying to be a writer and so he borrowed and Mom didn't know until after the war. We couldn't have kept on living in the brown bungalow anyway, even if Mrs. Weed hadn't sold it."

"But did Gramma want us?"

"Oh, yes. She suggested it. She said she was lonely."

"Will we ever be by ourselves, do you suppose?"

"Who knows?" He looked down into the water and she thought he'd retreated into himself, the way he could—into the private house of his head—and wasn't going to go on. And then, "But I can't keep asking about it. I haven't for a long time. The last time I said something Mom said it was no use and that she'd tell us when she was ready and we could start hunting."

Now they were both silent, looking back across the sparkling bay to the tiny wharves and buildings of San

Francisco on the far side, and the gulls swept steadily by, watching Julia's hand for it to begin tossing again.

Julia couldn't believe it. Her excited report to Gramma about Jennie dancing in the kitchen and how they'd all heard her, every one of them, even Aunt Alex, didn't prove a thing to Gram about animals having souls and going to heaven. Not a thing.

"But, *Gram*ma, don't you *see*? We wouldn't have *heard* her if she didn't have a soul and wasn't still alive somewhere. It *does* prove it—it *does*—"

The only thing that had saved Julia when first Patchy-cat and then Smokey had been run over, and then Georgie, her canary, had died, was the fact that they were still somewhere. The terrible part was that it had been her fault about Georgie. She'd begun letting him out of his cage to flutter around the room, and then he'd learned to come and perch on her bracelet, which so delighted her that she let him out more and more often, and would swing him in it and glide the bracelet, while he still perched there—happily, so it seemed—up and down through the air. After he died, someone, some neighbor, said it was because his heart had given out with too much flying; canaries couldn't take that much effort. They weren't used to it. So then guilt was added to grief, and the only thing she could think of that was the least morsel of comfort was that at least Georgie was in heaven.

But then Gramma said it was all tommyrot (her English way of saying it was all foolishness) and that Julia must face up to the fact that Patchy-cat and Smokey and Georgie were not among the Elect. No bird or animal was. It was not right or respectful to think they were.

"Oh, *Mother*—!" Mama had said, and Julia knew somehow that Mama, too, by her tone, was doubtful, but that she didn't want Julia's hopes smashed whether it was true or not about animal souls going on.

Julia had all this in her mind now while she and Gramma were talking about Jennie.

"Well, if people like that Mrs. Weed," she shouted suddenly, "just because she goes to church every Sunday, are going to get to go to heaven, but our darling cats and Georgie, who loved us and were so kind and beautiful, didn't go anywhere, just *stopped*, then I think God is hateful and horrible and mean. That's what I think!" And she glared at Gramma.

"Don't be blasphemous, child!" Gramma was appalled. "You point out to me one place in the Bible where it tells us that animals shall have life everlasting. Besides, how could Jennie's soul have claws that you could hear on the linoleum?"

"I don't know. Maybe it was magic. But you think Grandpa's in heaven, don't you?"

"Of course I do. And we shall be gathered together."

"And you heard him right after *he* died when he knocked on the veranda window. Didn't you?"

"What's that got to do with anything?" said Gramma suspiciously. She'd been twisted about and got into a corner by Julia before this.

"Well, how did his soul have knuckles to knock on the glass if you think Jennie's soul couldn't have claws to dance on the linoleum?"

"She's got you there, Gran," said Greg gravely, and Mama turned away suddenly and went into the bedroom.

"I don't know what's got into you people," cried Gramma, exasperated. "Jennie dancing on the linoleum when she's a week in her grave! I don't believe it for a second. And anyway, Grandpa was human, made in the image and likeness of God, and Jennie was nothing but a dog. And that's that."

Julia sat at the dining room table trying and trying to write about Jennie—just how she'd felt about her and just how it had all been when they heard her—using a piece of paper for now that she'd keep in Uncle Hugh's book. But she couldn't—she couldn't begin to. And she wrote and scratched out, and wrote and scratched. And the pencil lead was blunt and pale and her writing *was* awful. And the harder she tried the more awful it got, until suddenly, when the old unbearable burning pain rose from her chest into her throat, too big to hold back, she threw the pencil across the room and snatched up the paper and crushed it together in her fists and threw it onto the floor, struggling to keep back the tears. But her chest heaved and then the crying burst out and the acid tears overflowed just the way they had yesterday when she had had to cry about Jennie. And because she knew how she looked and how Greg was thinking what an abysmal nut she was, she put her head on her arms and cried onto the table. The thing was, it was as if she'd failed Jennie, as if there was nothing to be done with her love and everything she remembered, and then, too, as if it was utterly hopeless to try to write—because she was never, never going to be a writer after all, like her father.

"Oh, Julia," said Mama. And she came and sat down under the lamp next to her. "Julia!" and she slipped the back of her hand gently across the exposed arc of Julia's cheek. "Your face is scarlet—you're like a glowing ember."

"I know—I know. I should go jump in the bay and put myself out."

"So far as I can see," said Gramma, "there's no happiness in this sort of thing at all. None at all. You and your father!"

6

❧

The Cremation

Julia, with her precious journal still wrapped in its tissue paper and sumptuous ribbon, and a small box with a surprise in it for Maisie, sat on the Woollards' back porch at the top of the long flight of stairs that led up, under the kitchen windows, to their flat over a store. When Julia and Greg and Mama had lived in the brown shingled bungalow, Maisie Woollard and her parents had lived in a two-story brown house across the street and Maisie and Julia had become friends. But then something had happened. Greg said Mr. Woollard had lost his job, and they moved out of the two-story house into this flat facing on a busy street where the big orange trains thundered by every half hour. Not long after that the Redferns moved to Gramma's, her house luckily not far from the Woollards'.

"Bye bye, little lamb chop," murmured Julia to herself, her arms around her knees while she rocked thoughtfully. "Cham, cham, little bye lop. Bamb, bamb, little—" She and Maisie always had their fancy exits and entrances and Julia was thinking up a new exit, something to try out on Maisie. "Chye, chye, little—" And the screen door squeaked and twangled open, and she looked up at Mr. Woollard and snatched her book and box out of the way of his enormous feet.

"Oh, it's you," he said. "Heaven help!" He had his lunch pail and his big thick work boots on. He clumped down the stairs and twisted round. "Don't you go chivvying Maisie now 'til she's finished eating. You mind now. She'll be out when she's finished." And he went on down.

The Woollards were English, like Gramma and Mama and Uncle Hugh, but only Gramma said things like the Woollards. Mrs. Woollard called a napkin a serviette, the way Gramma did, and said that Maisie created, when she made a fuss. And once Julia heard Mr. Woollard say, "Where's me weskit?" and Mrs. Woollard handed him the vest to his suit. His waistcoat, Gramma said he meant.

Julia had never been sure about Maisie's father and mother, not sure, that is, that they liked her very much. She had a strong feeling somehow that they didn't, and just suffered her because she and Maisie were best friends.

Presently the kitchen window was run up and Mrs. Woollard looked out. She had bright pink cheeks and lots of frizzy dark hair and large ivory-colored teeth that sometimes clicked when she talked. "Oh, it's you—I thought I heard Mr. Woollard say something." Down went the window and after another longish wait, Maisie appeared at the back door.

"C'mon in," she said. Her lean legs and bony knees were encased neatly in long black stockings that never wrinkled, and her black hair was skinned right back into two tight braids with narrow ribbons that managed in some mysterious way always to stay tied. And though she invariably wore thickish underwear that showed here and there, she never seemed to get hot and red-faced like Julia.

"*Why* can't you stay neat and clean like Maisie!" Gramma would bitterly complain when Julia came home at dusk, damp, scuffed, battered about the knees, dirty-faced, her clothes sometimes torn, and with her hair a tangled mass that was practically impossible to comb without arousing screams of furious agony from Julia. "What gets into you!" Gramma would cry, vigorously working over Julia's hair while Julia hung onto it in desperation to try to abate the pain. "What in the name of Tophet do you *do,* Julia Redfern, to get into such a state!"

Julia hadn't any idea. She just lived, that was all. She and Maisie. But Maisie slipped sideways through the days instead of flying head-on the way Julia did, so that she emerged at the end of each one as spotless and unwrinkled as she'd gone in. Most of the time Julia never noticed the contrast between them, or thought much about it, except at hair-combing time. Then she hated Maisie.

Maisie took in the beautiful package and the box with eyes startlingly large in her white face. "Whatcha got?"

But Maisie had forgotten something: their Arpenglopish. "Harpellarpo, swarperthearpert."

"Harpellarpo," said Maisie dutifully, as Julia came into the dark little hall bearing her treasures.

"Wharpat arpe—I mean, arpare warpe—" began Julia.

"Oh, give over, *do!*" exploded Mrs. Woollard from the kitchen. She came out into the hall wiping her hands on a dishtowel. "Sometimes I think I'll go dotty listening to you two. What's all this?" and she nodded at Julia's possessions.

Suddenly it came to Julia that perhaps it wouldn't be at all wise to let Mrs. Woollard know what was in the little box, so she turned around, when she got into the living room, and put the box on the sofa, sat in front of it, and took the wrappings and ribbons off of Uncle Hugh's book. "This is my present from Uncle Hugh for my birthday. He had it made specially for me," and she held it up so that they could view with awe the gold-embossed cover and the dark rich green leather. Maisie and her mother stepped closer, but Mrs. Woollard had only to take one look when Julia opened it to show them the first page.

"What did he want to go and give you a fancy thing like that for? If you must scribble, he should have got you something like a ledger with ruled lines—you know the kind. Then if you make a mess, as you likely will, it wouldn't matter. But that'll never do. It's just money wasted, and a pretty penny it must have cost. Imagine!

Leather bound. And whatever will you put into it." Back she went to the kitchen.

Maisie sat down and took the book into her lap.

"Who wants to do all *that* writing!" she said finally, having flipped over the empty pages. And she clapped the book to and handed it back to Julia. "I *hate* writing. Imagine wanting to."

"Well, I do," said Julia fiercely, filled with humiliation and disappointment. Her magnificent present was as flat a failure as it could possibly be. "*I'm* going to be an author someday like my father and Louisa May Alcott."

"Who's she?" said Maisie. Julia examined her with disgust.

"You're the most hopeless person I've ever known in my whole life. In fact, you're positively bizarre."

At that moment Mrs. Woollard came in again, and Julia shifted herself back, nudging her box behind her into the pillow so that it should escape Mrs. Woollard's notice.

"Wharpat sharpall warpe darpo?" whispered Maisie as soon as her mother had gone into the bedroom. Maisie was very good at Arpenglopish.

Julia put her finger to her lips, nodded back toward the box, and narrowed her eyes in conspiracy. "*War*pait!" she hissed. She knew, and Maisie knew, that Mrs. Woollard would be going out to do her morning shopping.

"Now, then," said Mrs. Woollard coming in with her purse, "you do that dusting, Maisie Woollard, the way I told you. I'll be back in about an hour so you do a thorough good job and don't get into any mischief."

They waited until they heard Mrs. Woollard's footsteps grow faint and fainter down the back steps. She was gone—really gone. And Julia turned, drew forth the box, and opened it under Maisie's nose.

"A-a-a-ahg!" shrieked Maisie, flinging herself away. Then gingerly she leaned forward and had another look. "What did you want to go and bring that over for?" Julia said nothing, just sat there and smiled at her. "It's—it's dead, isn't it?"

"Of course it's dead, stupid. Stiff dead. It'd run out if it wasn't. And I thought we could cremate it and say a ceremony over it. I found it under a bush in the back yard. Feel, Maisie," and Julia gently stroked the mouse's silvery gray side, silky smooth, and ran her finger lightly down the pink, stiff tail, frozen into a little question mark. Its hind feet were drawn up and curled inward, like minute shriveled blossoms, and its front paws were pressed together as if in prayer. Its eyes were open, no longer bright, yet looking quite as if it were alive.

"What's cremate?"

"Good grief, you mean you never heard of cremating people?" Julia never had either until Greg had told her the other day. "You burn them up when they're dead and put what's left, the ashes, into an urn."

"What's an urn?"

"A big sort of vase, Greg says, with a cover on it."

"But we haven't got any urn. And why do you put them in that?"

"Oh, you just do," said Julia with enormous impatience, wanting to get on with the project and going over to the door.

"But then what do you do with the urn?"

66

The Cremation

"I don't know. Anyway, we'll put the rest of the mouse, the bones and things, into this box and bury it."

"But why not just bury the mouse the way it is?"

"Be*cause!*" Maisie really struck Julia at times as being the dullest creature imaginable about rich and beautiful possibilities. She just didn't seem to catch on at all. "Because it wouldn't be any fun, that's why! Now, come on—we have to find some sticks to make a fire."

"Do you just cook the mouse right in the fire?"

"Not cook, Maisie Woollard. *Cre*mate I *told* you—"

"But I've got to do the dusting."

"Well, come on, then, let's get it done," and Julia tossed down the mouse box, snatched up a doily from the couch arm, and went flicking rapidly around amongst all the other little doilies (Mrs. Woollard crocheted every evening, doily after doily after doily) and innumerable ornaments and pictures that covered every possible open space, while Maisie went about more carefully and deliberately, then disappeared into her parents' bedroom to finish off in there. When she got back Julia blew violently at the doily she'd used, beat it up and down on the couch a few times, then returned it, crooked, and gray and crumpled, to its usual place. Grabbing up the mouse box, she led the way along the hall and down the back steps.

But there were no sticks. The back yard, or what had once been a yard, was now entirely covered in cement—not a bush, not a tree, not a blade of grass remained, not even behind "Papa's garage." There was a covered dustbin, used by the store underneath the flat, and some piled cardboard boxes beside it. But when Julia picked one up with a view to tearing it into pieces, a head came out of the back door of the store. "Put that back, now, young one, and get along with you," bawled the store owner. "No scrounging around back there. We need those. Off with you!"

"Aren't there any newspapers in the garage?" Julia asked Maisie.

"No," said Maisie. "Besides, Papa keeps it locked. It's got some of our furniture in there."

They went out onto the sidewalk and looked up and down, then round to the front, and Julia went over onto the railroad tracks. "You come back, Julia Redfern. Mama has a fit if I go onto the tracks."

"Well, I'm not you," said Julia. But there was not a single stick and she came back. She was stumped. There was no going home to Gramma's, simply because of Gramma, who would not look with favor on the cremation of a mouse. And all at once she thought with longing of the brown house that now had the apartment building smashed up against its face. There would have been all sorts of sticks in that garden and perfect little secret corners where she and Maisie could have built their cremation fire and had their ceremony in complete privacy. Those were the days, thought Julia sadly and wistfully.

"*I* know," said Maisie excitedly when Julia got back to the sidewalk, "*I* know. We could cremate him in one of the saucepans, and then wash it good and proper. Couldn't we, Julia?" It seemed that Maisie wanted this cremation ceremony, and to view cremation with her very own eyes, just as fervently as Julia did.

"Hooray!" shouted Julia. "Of course!" And they pelted along the walk, around the corner to the back steps, and up into the Woollard kitchen. Down on their hands and knees in front of the pot cupboard, they clattered through it for what Julia thought would be "exactly right." When they'd found a nice heavy pan, they came up flushed and triumphant.

"Just put it there and light the gas," directed Julia, and she got out her stiff mouse and laid him reverently in the pan. Maisie had the gas very low. "Turn it up," said Julia. "We'll never get it cremated that way."

So Maisie turned the gas up full force. "Shouldn't we put a little water in?" she asked anxiously.

"We're not *cook*ing it, I told you." Now Julia closed her eyes, held her arms out over the stove, and was about to go into her ceremonial speech, "Dearly beloveds, we are gathered together here to do—" when there was the sound of the big orange train trying desperately to come to a halt, and then a crash, and cries. Maisie and Julia stood petrified for a breath or two, turned and gazed at each other, then pounded into the living room over to the windows and peered down, one at each window.

An automobile had been run into, and people were scurrying from all directions. There it was, slewed sideways on the tracks, with the orange train towering above it, and a man was getting out of the undamaged door. He seemed to be unhurt, and went around the other side of the train where the motorman was, and presently both men appeared, looking at the automobile and carrying on with angry disputation. Neither Julia nor Maisie could hear what they were saying, only the sound of their voices, back and forth. Both men made wide, indignant gestures, showing what each thought the other had done wrong and what he should have done. And now there was a crowd, and everybody appeared to be entering into the argument, telling everybody else what he had seen with his own eyes.

"Can you get yours up?" Julia had been tugging violently at her window, but not a thing happened.

"Nope. It's no use—the cords're broken." Maisie stopped. "O-o-oh, *Ju*—lia—the *mouse*—!"

Away went Maisie, Julia after her. For a ghastly stench, a fog, a thick and horrible miasma was invading the air, and just as they got to the stove and Maisie had grabbed up the pan, the back door banged and there was Mrs. Woollard. She threw her purse and grocery bags onto the table, strode over to Maisie and snatched the pan from her. When she'd stared into its depths, she threw it on the floor.

"What is it—what in the name of God—"

Maisie was struck dumb, her eyes enormous. She looked as if she were going to be sick, came into Julia's head, even as she herself was overcome with a wild compulsion to get out—get out the door and down the back steps and away. "It's a mouse," she said, but faintly. "It's only a dead mouse, Mrs. Woollard. We were —we were cremating it, but then there was a crash out front, and we—"

"A *mouse*—! And you've *ruined* my best saucepan—" Mrs. Woollard pinned them with blazing eyes. "My very best heavy saucepan I do pot roasts in and that, the only decent one I've got, the one I've had for fifteen years from the Old Country—a wedding present, it was, and I can't get another like it. A mouse—charred to a crisp—cooked—with all its hairs—and the pan's black—"

Suddenly she clutched Maisie with both hands and shook her by the shoulders until Maisie's head bobbled. "*Smell* this place—just *smell* it! I'll never get it out of here, nor the black off that pan. It's ruined—as if I don't have enough trying to make ends meet—and you, Julia Redfern—" Here she rounded on Julia. "It's one thing after another with you. You get out of here this instant and never come back, d'you understand? Never!"

Julia got herself into the hall, escaped onto the porch, and rattled down the steps, but she was no more than halfway when she remembered Uncle Hugh's book. She poised there, heart thudding, knowing there was no going another inch without her book. Now cries issued from the kitchen—Maisie was being spanked. "But it wasn't *me*, Mama—it wasn't *me*—Julia said—" More cries, and Julia crept up, crept past the kitchen, nipped into the living room, got her book, tiptoed quickly back to the door and down the stairs again, around the corner and onto the main street, then tore along toward home as fast as she could go. And it wasn't just me. It wasn't. It was Maisie said that about getting her mother's saucepan. I'd never have thought of it—cremating a mouse in a saucepan! Oh, golly, what'll Gramma say if she ever finds out—

"Well, what's got into you, young one?" inquired Gramma, plucking up a fistful of flour from the flour bin and dropping it into the mixing bowl, then a bit more, then tossed in some baking powder and salt, cut in some lard, then poured in the milk. She was making dumplings to go with the chicken stew, Julia's utmost favorite dinner, besides beef and Yorkshire pudding, which they had on special occasions. Only Hulda could make as good a Yorkshire pudding as Gramma, and Gramma never seemed to measure anything when she cooked. A fistful of this, and a pinch or so of that, she always said.

But there'd be no relishing chicken and dumplings tonight. For Julia felt the old nagging in her stomach she knew so well—guilt and worry, this time. Other times, bitter disappointment.

"I said, what's got into you?" persisted Gramma, slanting a sharp little eye at Julia.

"Nothing."

"Don't tell *me*! You fall and crack your head again? You better tell me, whatever it is. No use letting it go— we'll find out sooner or later."

She meant the time Julia had fallen off the acting bar, the highest one, when she was showing off doing spins, hooking a leg over, grasping the bar with both hands, then going round and round and round—only, one hand slipped and that's all she knew until she came to in somebody's house with her cheek all swollen and a black eye and a dull, nagging pain in her head. But she said nothing about the pain, being afraid she'd never get to go on the acting bar again, and after a while it went away. Julia was sure though, even now, that she could feel little lumps in her cheek—buried gravel.

As soon as Mama got home: "Julia, go into the bedroom. I have something to say to you." By the look on her face,

and the tone of her voice, Julia knew at once that somehow, in what way she couldn't guess, Mama had heard
about the mouse. "Sit down," Mama pointed to the bed,
and while Julia sat, looking sideways, toes crossed, and
her hands gripped together in her lap, Mama came and
stood at the foot. "I saw Mrs. Woollard on the way home
from work. She'd forgotten something at the grocers and
when I went in, she was there." Mama stopped and
studied her. "Julia, how could you do such an unspeak-
able thing! Her pan, that expensive pan, absolutely
ruined!"

"Well, it *isn't* absolutely ruined. I've been thinking.
She could have scraped it."

Mrs. Redfern raised her eyes to heaven. "You could
not scrape off charred, burned mouse. Not with all those
hairs. And do you think that even if she *could* scrape and
polish that pan, she'd ever use it for food again? Oh,
the stench must have been frightful. Mrs. Woollard said
her husband was furious when he got home, and that
she'd spanked Maisie. She thought you deserved a spanking too, a jolly good one, but of course, she said, she had
no control over that."

Julia could just hear Mrs. Woollard letting fly with
her opinions.

"Are you going to?"

"No, I'm too tired. Besides, I'm not at all sure it would
do any good. But I'll tell you one thing. I paid Mrs.
Woollard for that pan, and now you can pay me." Julia
stared at her mother in shocked amazement. "I suppose
you've spent all your Christmas money, so I'll put a bill
in the drawer. And you can just sit here until dinner and

think how you can be more useful than you have been. Is the table set?" Julia nodded. "Sometimes you're too much for me, Julia Redfern. You weary me to the bone, you really do, and that's the truth of the matter." And she went out and closed the door behind her.

Julia flopped back on the bed, stared up at the ceiling for a moment or two, then hoisted her legs and began pedaling. Aunt Alex at the table: "Oh, it's our word girl again. Oh, dear, oh, dear—you're marvelous, Julia. Sight-sore! Ha, ha, ha. Ho, ho, ho." And everybody looks at Julia, and Julia, very calm and dignified, in a perfect little space of silence so that everyone can hear clearly, "Aunt Alex, you weary me to the bone, you really do, and that's the truth of the matter."

7

I, Julia Caroline Redfern

But it so happened that Gramma, the next morning, after Mrs. Redfern left for work, was out in front talking to a neighbor when she saw Mrs. Woollard up at the corner. Both being English, they'd become friendly when the Woollards lived across from the Redferns, and Gramma would drop by. Now Mrs. Woollard told her everything that had happened and Gramma came charging back, burning with indignation. If Maisie had gotten a spanking, she said, Julia deserved one.

"But you'd have no right!" exclaimed Julia, backing away.

"Oh, wouldn't I!" cried Gramma. "After watching out for you for three solid years, bedeviled by you and suffering over you! I'd have a right, young lady, and don't you forget it. If your mother didn't have the strength, I do. Not a peep did I hear out of that bedroom last night when she took you in there to talk to you, about what, she wouldn't say. But somebody's got to teach you right from wrong or you'll grow up like that father of yours. Not a thought for anybody but himself did he have, not a grain of consideration. Never said he was sorry for anything, not once, to me *or* your mother no matter what he did or said, idling his time away day after day, scribbling, while your mother went out to work, and not a thing accomplished, not a penny coming in from him. Then off he'd go again on one of his grand schemes for putting your mother on Easy Street. That was a fine joke that was— Easy Street! Then back he'd come to be waited on hand and foot, and not to be disturbed, he wasn't. Oh, no, not him. A writer, *he* was. He might not earn a living, but *he* was His Lordship—"

"Well he was!" shouted Julia. "I mean he *was* a writer. And I'm going to be one too, the minute I can get my desk back—"

"Ah!" said Gramma, a red spot blazing in each cheek and the tip of her nose red and her little eyes crackling. "Well, then, heaven help you. Because you'll never make a cent out of it. And heaven help you for being just like him in other ways—thoughtless and selfish and stubborn. P'raps you didn't know your mother had to waste good hard-earned money paying Mrs. Woollard for that confounded pot—"

"Yes, I know—I *know* that. And I'm going to pay Mama. I said I would—"

"How, I'd like to know," retorted Gramma. "With what—an expensive pan like that!"

"Well, you'll see. You'll just see. I've got it all planned. I *will* pay her."

But when she got to the library she did not, after all, go into the Children's Room and put her question to Mrs. Coates as she'd planned to do. No. All joy and expectation spent, and overcome with her own foolishness, she hung about in the main hall staring up at the bulletin boards. When people came in from outside, the heavy doors went "whoof" behind them, and they climbed up the broad stairway to the grown-ups' department, or other kids came in and went right into Children's because all they wanted was books.

Julia had known Mrs. Coates since she was five when Mama had brought her here to get her own card, but Mrs. Coates said she was very sorry, Julia had to be six, and Julia let out such a howl of insult and disappointment as must have been heard all over the library. "But I can read!" she sobbed. "I can read!" It made no difference. The rules had to be followed. No card.

And thinking what a mere silly child she'd been in that far-off time, she wondered suddenly if she should go upstairs and see the head librarian for such a question as hers. Maybe Mrs. Coates wasn't the one. But that would be far worse, and Julia girded her loins and marched determinedly into Children's, laced her way among the tables and chairs, and stood waiting at Mrs. Coates's desk while she stamped out a pile of books.

Mrs. Coates was majestic like Aunt Alex, but not so large. She, too, had rather a full bust on which necklaces swooped and swung, and sometimes, when she forgot herself on arriving in the morning, went right to her work —she was apt to be absentminded about some things— and would still have her hat on by midmorning. She had red-gold hair done up into a large roll on top of her head, and by afternoon wisps would begin to escape. But she never bothered about them and would smile at you through her down-sloping eyeglasses and give you all sorts of suggestions about books you might not have read or about new ones that had just come in.

Finally she lifted to Julia her kind blue eyes. "Hello, dear. What can I do for you? Have you run out of reading matter?" Julia was often tickled by some of the things Mrs. Coates said; it was just like her to say reading matter instead of books. "Or have you written something you would like me to see?"

Julia shook her head. Her hands were cold, and now her heart quickened, not because she was scared of asking Mrs. Coates, but scared of being turned down. "Mrs. Coates, you know the boy who puts the books away?"

"Yes, dear. Corky, the page. 'Shelving,' we call it."

"Well, does he work all the time?"

"Oh, no, just a few hours a week."

"Well, I was wondering—do you suppose I could work a few hours a week too, putting away the books he doesn't have time to? I would be very good at it."

"I know you would, Julia. I know that. But he gets everything done. He's very quick. You see, he comes in for an hour or two a day and works two or three hours on Saturdays. And that's about all we need."

Yes. She'd had a feeling all along, underneath, that it

would be hopeless. It had been too perfect an idea, too perfectly the kind of job she would rather have had than any other—something to do with books, with this room, this very special place.

"You don't need anybody to dust?"

Mrs. Coates gazed at her in amazement. "Do you want to dust, Julia? Do you like it?"

"Oh, no. I hate, loathe, and detest it. But I want a job."

Mrs. Coates leaned her elbows on the desk, folded her hands and rested her chin on them. "The thing is, Julia," and she looked genuinely regretful—but then you never felt she was just putting on or being polite, "the thing is, I'm afraid you're too young to get a job here. Corky's fourteen, and we have a janitor, you see, who does all the cleaning and dusting, upstairs and down. If it were up to me, I would surely think of something you might do. But it isn't up to me."

Julia could find no answer, only stared at Mrs. Coates's desk with all its fascinating objects—stamps and stamp pad, desk blotter, holder for pens and pencils, boxes of clips, long wooden boxes of cards that Mrs. Coates had to nibble through to find the right ones to put into the book pockets when you returned your books, another box with a lot of fresh book pockets in case some should be torn or dirty—all sorts of important and satisfying things. And it reminded Julia once again of her own desk her father had made her, which she yearned for. But there was no room for it in Mama's and her tiny bedroom so that it had been stored with the rest of their furniture.

"Thank you, Mrs. Coates." And Julia wandered away along the wall by the fairy tales, but she didn't feel in the least like reading, not even one of her favorites, Hans Andersen's *Fairy Tales*, *The Yellow Fairy Book*, or *The Blue* or *The Green*, or *The Japanese Book of Fairy Tales*, or *The Tales of King Arthur*.

Usually, in this room of all places, she was perfectly content, this room with its cool, greenish-gold light filtering in through the vines and trees outside, and its richly dark paneling and the tall grandfather clock standing between the Ernest Thompson Seton books on one side and the beginning of the nature books on the other. It was usually rather still in here, with the grandfather clock going tock, tock, tock, tock, slow and lazy and solemn.

She always thought of this room as being cozy, perhaps because of the low ceiling—upstairs the big main room was enormous with a great high ceiling she felt lost under. On hot days like this it was heavenly to come in here from the outside glare, and on rainy days it was cozier than ever to sit in the soft orangey light and be vaguely aware of the rain dripping against the windows while Mrs. Coates spoke in a low voice to other children. You could go on blissfully reading and there was nobody to bother you or to shriek at you to come and wipe the dishes or to clean up your mess. Gramma couldn't stand seeing anybody laxing around when there was something that needed doing, even if it could have been done some other time.

Julia scudded along Shattuck, headed for the music store, and when she arrived,

"Julia, where are you going?" Celia Redfern was sailing past the counter with a stack of records she was taking to one of the little booths where people listened before they chose what they wanted to buy. The booths had big glass windows and you could see the people sitting in there, leaning on their crossed-over knees and staring into space with no expressions.

"Downstairs. Into the basement." She was going to play Dungeon, locked up forever down there with the rats that had made their nests under the piled-up boxes and packing cases and mounds of excelsior.

"Wait—there's something I'd like you to do."

But there were still three people lined up at the counter, so Julia opened the basement door and turned and closed it behind her. She listened, and in the cold, evil-smelling dark, heard rustlings and scuttlings, and now two luminous green points stared up at her from the bottom of the stairs, then vanished. Mama said she'd seen a rat as big as a cat down there. ("Oh, Mom!" said Greg, but Uncle Hugh said he'd seen one as big as a dog, kept in a cage at the London docks.) They had their tunnelings through from the basement of the Greek restaurant next door, and no matter how many traps Mr. Stanhope, the manager of the store, put around or how cleverly he poisoned various kinds of bait, he could not stem the tide.

I dare you, Julia Redfern, to go all the way to the bottom without turning on the light. I dare you to stand there in the dark and count to fifty. But once, even with the light on, a rat had run across Mama's feet. Now the basement door opened.

"Julia?"

"Gramma wanted to spank me," said Julia, looking up at her. "Because of Mrs. Woollard. She told Gramma everything, and Gramma says I'm just like my father, selfish and thoughtless, and that he never earned a penny or said he was sorry about anything, but always came back from being away and expected to be waited on. She called him His Lordship and said heaven help me for wanting to be like him."

"Gramma said that to *you*?" The strangest expression came over Celia Redfern's face. "Well, come up now, and I'll tell you what I'd like you to do." And when they came up into the light of day Mama handed her a package that Julia knew contained records. "Dr. Jacklin phoned and wants these for tonight, but the repair man's already left so there's nobody to take them. Now, you know Oak Grove Park, Julia. You go up along this side of it halfway, and his street is right there, Live Oak Lane. You've passed it dozens of times. I've written it right on the package, 226 Live Oak. And, Julia, listen to me. Do not go into the park and forget what you're up there for and leave the records. Do you hear me? Can I trust you? I would like very much to be able to trust you."

Julia looked at her mother sternly. "I promise," she said. "I faithfully and sincerely promise that you can trust me."

She knew the way to the park so well that there was no need to think of the turnings as she climbed toward the hills. In the hot, dry heat—"What an unusual summer!" everybody said—she lost herself in her "seeing." And it was her father she saw, his feet, going back and forth, back and forth, amongst the blackberry vines in the garden of the brown bungalow while she crouched in her cave of leaves where she always hid when he "went all dark."

He'd gotten after her, but what had she done? She couldn't remember. She'd run off from him to her secret hideout and presently he came out of the house and began marching up and down the way he would when one of his manuscripts came back. That's what they were called, she'd known even then, those piles of paper he wrote his stories on. And they often did come back in their tan envelopes, she noticed, and if Mama got the mail ahead of him and a big envelope was there, she'd look around as if trying to escape from it.

But there was no escape and when her father found out that his story wasn't wanted, he'd bang out of the house into the garden and not answer when Mama called him for dinner.

Other times, when he was in the midst of his writing, he was happy, and would take her and Greg for long walks in the hills when he was through working, and tell them stories about when he'd been a boy. Sometimes they were so funny—nobody could tell stories like her father had. The strange part was, he'd tell them only when they'd walk in the hills or down toward the bay across the huge fields where the cows were. Those cows! She'd have been afraid of them alone but not when the three of them went uncaring through herd after herd right down to the tarry-smelling wharves, where her father bought bags of little pink crisp shrimps out of the steaming barrels in front of the sheds for them to eat on the way home.

When he got something accepted they would celebrate. He would take them out to dinner at some special place, and one of those times he'd bought paint and they'd painted all the rooms of the brown bungalow. Even Julia was given a brush, and her father showed her how to put on the paint without slopping, a little at a time.

She stood in the middle of the sidewalk, her face hot, the package beginning to be heavy under her arm, seeing her father painting and singing while he painted, then turning and grabbing up Mama and spinning her around and around. She looked up, and already she was opposite the park—she couldn't believe it! And she was about to cross the street to where Live Oak turned off to the right when she heard something, a soft, small fluttering, down low, nearby. Then it stopped, then started up again with a kind of steady desperation.

She knelt down—yes, yes, it was right here in this bush. Gently she parted the branches and peered in, and in a stroke of sunlight saw a brown bird with a pinkish-red face and breast that stared up at her with wide terrified eyes and gaping beak while more desperately than ever it tried to get free. But free from what? And she slipped her hand in among the branches and took hold of the soft, palpitating body and lifted it up and saw that a hair was wound around one of its legs. In a second, perhaps two, she had the hair unloosed and drew the bird out, held up her hand and opened her fingers—and with a single strange cry it was gone. She stood quiet, seeking for where it had vanished into the tree over her head, but she did not see it again.

She was overcome with wonderment.

I have saved a life. I, Julia Caroline Redfern, have saved a life. What a miraculous turn of fate it had been that, just as she came to this spot and almost passed by but not quite, she should have stood here to see her father being happy and to think about him, right at this bush where the bird was caught and, standing still, was able to hear that tiny flutter. A lot of children together would have been yelling and shouting. Grown-ups would be too far up to have heard it. But she had heard. It was like a fairy tale. Perhaps the bird was magical and was testing her. Perhaps it hadn't been a bird at all but a prince or an old witch or a magician in the guise of a bird. Who knew what would happen now, what twist of fate awaited?

8

———◆———

Dr. Jacklin

Halfway along Live Oak she came to a stone wall where an old bent man was hosing down the walk with a positive Niagara of water. Perhaps he would look up at her from under his hairy brows and say, "So you freed the bird. Good. That was the first test. Now come with me." But he didn't. When he looked up he said, "Ye always gotta worsh it off with a hunnert pounds pressure—otherwise ye don't get the leaves."

"Is this—?" began Julia, and saw the numbers, 226, set into the stone wall in gold metal shapes.

And went empty and sick. The records—where were they? What had she done with them? On trembling legs that scarcely held her she ran back the way she had come. What had she done—what had she done? She couldn't think—couldn't remember. She had had them, and then hadn't. And when she turned the corner of Live

Oak and raced downhill toward the bush where she'd freed the bird, the package was gone.

What shall I *do*—? and she got down and scrabbled under the bush and searched along the fence beneath the dusty hedge. "Oh, but I promised—I promised! Oh, Mama—" and the hot tears squeezed out and ran down her scarlet face, and she dashed them away and stood up and heard footsteps coming along the walk behind the fence, behind the high hedge.

"Child?" Julia held a sob in midbreath and a woman appeared at the corner of the hedge with the package in her hands, and came toward Julia holding it out. "I was in there doing my gardening, and I heard you talking—saying something about a bird. And when I came out later to clip the hedge, you were gone, but I found your package and not knowing where you'd run off to, I thought I'd keep it for you until you came back, for fear somebody would take it."

Oh, she was happy. Everything was all right, because the bird hadn't been a bird, but someone powerful in disguise, just as she'd expected. And she'd been saved. And when she came to the old bent man again he looked up and winked at her as if he knew something he wasn't telling. She turned in under the stone archway and started up the stone steps, and the old man called out to her, "A hunnert'n ten of 'em an' I bet you don't get to the top without stopping to catch yer breath. But *I* can—" and he chuckled and went on with his hosing. "All at one go—"

Julia laughed to herself and went running up, turn after turn, all hidden under layers and thickets of greenery where scratchings and rustlings could be heard among the dead leaves. And there was one bird that kept breaking into a bright, complex ripple of notes, very pure and clear, that you couldn't begin to follow as you could the other birds' pipings and callings.

By the time she got to the top where the steps opened out onto a courtyard of flagstones she was singing to herself, "And the clock—stopped—never to go again—when the old—man—*died*!" And stood there taking it all in: the beds of ferns and flowers and the picnic table with books and the remains of a meal on it, and an old hat, and papers lifting in a hot little puff of wind. The house up above stood on stilts on this side because of the steepness of the hill, and wound away up the side of it as she'd never seen a house do, this way and that, all windows, it seemed, that reached to the floor, the most curious house that ever was with ferns and other green things planted in underneath. And there were three creamy cats with dark ears and dark faces, except for creamy patches below their ears, sitting at one of the broad windows looking down at her.

"I believe," said a voice, "that that jingle started when the clock actually did stop at the moment some emperor died. Now which one was it? I knew, seems to me. Yes—Frederick the Great."

A long stork of a man with bushy white hair and dark brows and a beaky nose like Greg's stood up from where he'd been digging or weeding or planting, and pressed a hand to either side of his back and let out a groan. "Oh, age, age! The only difference between old Barty and me is that I can stand up straight, but hurt when I garden.

And he can't stand up straight, but never hurts, and that's not fair because he's five years older than I am."

"He said there's a hunnert'n ten steps and that he bet I couldn't get to the top without stopping to catch my breath but he can—"

"And did you?"

Julia put the records on the picnic table. "No," she said. "Once I had to stop." Even if she'd wanted to, there would be no use fibbing, even if no one saw her to know the truth, because of the bird. She was sure it had its eye on her. "Are you Dr. Jacklin?"

"Yes, and you're Julia. Your mother phoned to say you were coming." He fished in his pocket. "What's your lucky number?"

"Ten—at least I think it is."

"And my lucky number's three, and three times ten is thirty, so this is for Julia, who huffed and puffed my records all the way up from Shattuck in the heat."

"*Thirty cents?*"

"Yes, is that all right? Is that enough?"

"Oh, yes." Julia folded the three dimes in her palm. "It's magic. And all because of my rescuing the bird. I knew something good would happen. You see, I owe Mama because of the cremated mouse."

"The cre—? Well, look, Julia, why don't we go up and have some lemonade and cookies and you can say hello to the cats, and we can talk for a bit. What I want to know is: why is it magic my giving you the thirty cents, and what has the bird to do with it?"

As they went up, Julia told him about the bird caught by a human hair and how marvelous it was that she

should have been standing right there at that special spot
thinking about her father and so was able to hear the tiny
flutter of the bird trying to get free. "I thought it was like
the youngest son in the fairy tale—you know, being
tested, but he doesn't know it, and does a good deed just
because he wants to, and then something tremendous
happens. He's saved, or he finds a fortune, or gets the
princess. I thought perhaps the bird wasn't a bird at all,
but an old witch in disguise, or a prince, or maybe a
magician."

"Ah," said Dr. Jacklin. "Yes, one never knows, does
one?" And when they'd got to the door and he'd opened
it and they went in, "Now," he said, "I want you to meet
my three Siamese daughters, Sukhothoi, whom I call
Sookie, and Ananda who is called just Nanda, and Timka,
their mother. Timka's the heavy one with the green eye."

For a moment the three creamy cats, with their dark
brown ears and faces and legs and tails, turned their
heads to study Julia with intent, measuring, luminous
blue eyes and the one green one. Then Timka got up—
"Mung-g-o-o-w?" she inquired, and approached with
dignity, tail aloft. Whereupon Sookie trotted forward and
got to Julia first.

"Mung-g-o-o-w?" asked Sookie.

"Mung-gow," said Nanda, remaining where she was.

Julia knelt down and put her cheek against Timka's,
and got strenuously rubbed and pushed against, while
Sookie came nosing in under Julia's arm. "The Three
Mung-gows," said Julia, enchanted. "That's what they
are, Dr. Jacklin. Is it what you call them?"

"Why, I'd never thought of it, I'll have to confess,

though that is most certainly their word. But from now on it's Timka, Sookie, and Nanda Mung-gow. As you can see, Nanda tends to be a bit standoffish. There she goes, up onto the mantle—but notice how delicate and precise she is. She never upsets a thing. That's where she likes to sit and view strangers. She studies and watches, and then if she gets to know you and approves of you, you just may be allowed to touch her, but I can't promise. Now, you come along out here and wash your poor hot face and your rather grubby paws and I'll be squeezing some lemons."

Her rather grubby paws! Nobody, not even Mrs. Coates, had ever called them that, but so they were. She liked Dr. Jacklin. And when they were settled where they could look out through the trees at glimpses of Berkeley and the bay and a far-off San Francisco, and The Three Mung-gows had bunched down onto their tucked-under paws, prepared to listen to the conversation, Dr. Jacklin said, "Now about the cremated mouse, Julia. Who cremated it and why do you owe money because of it?"

So Julia told him, and the awful way it had all turned out, and how Mama had paid Mrs. Woollard for the ruined pan, and that Julia was to pay *her*, though just how wasn't yet known, "but at least now I have thirty cents."

"Ah," said Dr. Jacklin. "You know, Julia, my old Barty just won't weed. The older he gets the more ornery and bossy he gets, and I have an idea he hates weeding though he won't admit it, and says it's because he can't kneel anymore. But he can do all sorts of other things, I notice. At any rate, I wonder if you would like to take on the job. Are you a good weeder?"

Julia looked down at Timka and Sookie, who returned her gaze steadily, and, she thought, rather searchingly: *A good weeder!* "We-e-ell," she said finally, "I haven't done much weeding. But if I could earn some money, I guess maybe I'd better." (She could feel Gramma's eye on her when she'd said, "And I'm going to pay Mama—" "How, I'd like to know—with what?" demanded Gramma. "You'll see. You'll just see. I've got it all planned—") "Shall I begin this instant?"

"Oh, Lord, no, not yet. Let's rest for a bit. What's all this about your grandma wanting to give you a whacking? Do you often get whacked?"

So then Julia told him all about Gramma, and how she favored Greg— "In fact, she's positively fatuous about him, the way Aunt Alex is, but certainly not about me, and it could be because I'm too much like my father, who was a writer. But Gramma thinks there's no use or future in that, because writers hardly earn a penny, she says. But I don't care. I'm going to be one anyway."

"Have you ever written anything, or is this just an idea you have?"

"Well, it's sad. You see Uncle Hugh gave me the most beautiful book bound in green leather with my name stamped in gold on it and *The Private Journal of Julia Redfern* inside on the first page. But I can't write in it. I can't, even though I've tried. I mean I've tried to start. But it's no use—"

"You're intimidated—"

"What's—?"

"Made afraid, uncertain, anxious, because the book is too magnificent—"

"Yes, that's it exactly! And I don't know what I'm going to tell Uncle Hugh. He'll be hideously disappointed, because he had the book made 'specially for me, and I'll bet Aunt Alex had a fit. But he always wants to think up something just right. He wanted to give Greg a brand-new typewriter and though I'll bet Aunt Alex wouldn't have minded, Mama wouldn't hear of it. So he had a secondhand one fixed up as good as new and now Greg's started to write his Egyptian book on it, but he won't let me touch it. Anyway, I thought because I loved Jennie so much—she was Uncle Hugh's collie—that I'd write something special about all of us hearing her dance in the kitchen even though she'd been dead for a week. So I tried but it was no use, and I got into a state."

Dr. Jacklin looked a bit boggled at this point. "You heard Jennie dancing—and she's been dead for a week?"

"Oh, yes—all of us, though Aunt Alex wouldn't admit she heard. But I happen to know she did."

"Extraordinary! Tell me, Julia. How did you know?"

"Why, because of her expression. She didn't fool me. She just doesn't like anything you can't explain. She never has."

"I see. Now tell me this. Your father had a hard go of it, being a writer?"

"Yes, he did—"

"Well, then, why do you want to be one?"

"I don't know. I just do. I'm always thinking how something could be a story. And then he made my desk for me before he had to go away to France, the most beautiful desk you've ever seen, with drawers and everything. And Gramma couldn't understand it. She said it should have been for Greg, and why did he want to go making a great big thing like that for a mere child, and where would we put it? But he told her that I was going to be a writer, and that I would need it. And I *am* going to be one, though I certainly wish I could have my desk. But I can't. There's no room for it, not in Gramma's house there isn't."

Dr. Jacklin seemed to study the situation. "You know, I have something I think you could use—" He got up and went out of the room and when he came back he had a long gray book. He opened it and Julia saw that it was what Gramma used to keep accounts in: a ledger, the pages ruled with blue lines, and with red ones down the right-hand side where she did her adding.

"Why, that's what Mrs. Woollard, Maisie's mother, said I should have instead of Uncle Hugh's book."

"I think she was right, Julia—just for now. In this book —it's an old one and I had to tear out some pages—you can let yourself go. It won't matter how you write. And you can try your story about Jennie again, nice and easy and relaxed. Don't worry. Forget about yourself trying to be a writer."

Julia took the ledger onto her lap, flipping over the pages. "When I go to bed at night, or almost any time— but especially then, I can think of anything I want, just as if it was real. And I can see it happening."

Dr. Jacklin smiled. "Yes, I have an idea you can. Now let's go down and see what kind of weeder you are, then

I can get on with what I'm supposed to be doing—working on a paper I have to deliver."

"A newspaper? Just one?"

Dr. Jacklin got a kick out of that. "I mean I have to give a lecture—a talk. And funny as it may seem, that's called 'delivering a paper.'"

9

Some Private Notes

Dear Jennie,

Dr. Jacklin gave me this good pencil along with the ledger, because he said it helps to have one with just the right point and not too soft or too hard. My other old pencil was so pale and hard, it made everything worse so maybe I can put down what I want this time.

When I got through weeding a flower bed it was lunchtime and so we had lunch at the picnic table. That was Dr. Jacklin's breakfast that was there and he took it away and then we ate and I told him about you and just how everything happened. I told him about the little yelp you would give when you were excited and your nails clicked on the linoleum and on the bare floor in the hall when you danced on your hind legs for joy and I asked him if you could really have been there and he said he didn't know.

I asked him if he thought animals went to heaven and that Gramma said they didn't. And he said not someplace up in the sky but just part of life everywhere and that's all he would say. I think he didn't want to say anymore because of Gramma.

Well a part of life everywhere isn't so bad but I'd a lot rather you were your own self Jennie just exactly the way you were and I asked Dr. Jacklin if you were *not* just your own self somewhere but part of everything all over the place how you could have yelped and danced and we could hear you. He said he didn't know or about Mama and Uncle Hugh hearing Grandpa knock on the window on his funeral night or Mama seeing Uncle Artie at the foot of her bed when he'd been killed. But he says it's no use worrying about all the things we can't explain.

I asked him if I wanted it hard enough if maybe you would come and dance for me and let out your little bark and he said he didn't really think so and that I musn't count on things like that. But I just want to tell you Jennie that if you ever feel like it I would love to see you or just hear you dancing the way you used to for Hulda when she had your bowl for you and you looked so beautiful on your hind legs with your tail waving and your paws up in front and I wouldn't be a bit scared if I heard you. Only don't come when Gramma is here because I don't think she would like it.

Love from Julia

———◆———

I feel better now because of the money from weeding. You should have seen Gram's face. She didn't know what

to say because she never believed I could earn any money, and I told her I am going to go right on weeding until the flower beds and all the ferns under the house are finished. School starts in two weeks and maybe by then I can pay back what I owe.

◆

I hate loath and despise weeding almost as much as I do dusting that I thought was the worst thing in the world. Once or twice I almost wished I'd never taken up the records to Dr. Jacklin's but then I'd never have met him and The Three Mung-gows. I love them and wouldn't have missed them for anything, the way we can talk back and forth and they come and sit in the flower beds and watch what I'm doing or run up and down the trees and chase each other around and it's so entertaining that sometimes Dr. Jacklin has to come down and take them in because I don't get on with the weeding.

Sometimes I think I will never finish because I hate it so, but then I think about Gram and her not believing I can do anything. She doesn't say a word when I put my money from what I've done at Mama's place at the table. And that makes me half mad and half laughing it's so funny about Gram. Once she said well we'll see how it all turns out when Mama said "Haven't you anything to say to Julia?"

◆

I had a dream last night about Gramma. She looked different than the way she really is. Her back was curved up at her shoulders so she seemed like a bird with hardly any neck. And in the dream I was in front of the mirror in her bedroom trying to pull my neck down and curve my back, to bunch myself like Gram, and she saw me. What in the name of heaven are you doing, Julia? and I said, Being you, Gramma, to see how it feels to have a bunched back, and her mouth opened and her eyes sparked at me and she cried, Cruel! Cruel! How can you be so cruel! And I never meant to be cruel to her but was only trying to imagine how it felt to be all bunched up like her the way she was in the dream.

◆

The best part about everything is when after a while Dr. Jacklin calls to me when he's finished working to come up and have some lemonade, and then we sit there and talk to The Mung-gows and I've worked out what their language is, and Dr. Jacklin agrees.

mung-gow means hello

prrrowww? and *miaaaa?* and *mrrrrf? mrrrrf?* they say when they're about to be fed, and then

mrru, mrrrru, mrru (not *mew* or *meow*) very quick and contented and joyous when the food is put down

eeeeeowwww! when they're shut out and unhappy, or *meeeeep!* very pitiful

mrrrrr? when they come running in from outside and are announcing themselves, or are hidden in the ferns and I come by *mmmrrrrrrrrowwww,* kind of hollow and sad and long. I don't know what this means. I've only seen Nanda do this, and she stands hunched up and sounds like a strange cat—wild, when she does it. It seems to come from the middle of her stomach.

———◆———

Dr. Jacklin has taken me all over his house and it's the most wonderful and strange house I've ever seen. It is long and kind of winding. You don't go around in a circle the way you do in most houses, but along from one room to another in a crooked line and the house climbs up the hill so that is why there are stairs now and then and why it is on stilts on one side of it with the ferns underneath. And this way there can be windows on both sides of the rooms looking out into the trees, big long windows so that you feel you're outside all the time and I should think Dr. Jacklin would feel he's sleeping in the woods. He's lucky to have this house and The Three Mung-gows. And old Barty.

There are deep colored rugs on the floor in the living room that he says are Persian and in his bedroom he has matting that smells like a hot field in the sun and I love it and want it in my bedroom when I have one because of the delicious smell. And there are the strangest pictures on the walls that he says are what the painters painted and are not prints and some are famous. He bought them when he was in France when he was young with his wife who is dead now and that was the happiest time of his life. She has been dead for three years but she lived in this house for a little while. He built it for her just the way she wanted it. Dr. Jacklin has two deep creases down his cheeks, one on each side and because of this and his eyes he looks sad sometimes but when I asked him he said, No, no, not at all. I was sad at first but not now. Everything is all right.

I don't understand the pictures. Some I can see what they are and some I can almost but not quite and it's a puzzle. Dr. Jacklin's house is the one I would most like to live in even more than Uncle Hugh's and Aunt Alex's because of the trees and the windows and the good smell and because it is so strange, but comfortable even though it is like living in the branches of a tree.

Oh yes the weeding is worth it, in fact I know it is and I don't mean the money.

◆

Hulda *did* hear Jennie! Uncle Hugh phoned Mama at the music store today and said that Hulda came to him when Aunt Alex was out. She said she had to make a confession and told him she'd lied about Jennie because she knew what Aunt Alex would say and how Aunt Alex would tease her. On my birthday night she'd been thinking so hard about Jennie after I found out what happened that all at once when she heard the sound of her claws on the linoleum she completely forgot Jennie was dead and turned around to speak to her and then remembered and couldn't believe she wasn't there. She was going to go into the dining room to tell us but when she got to the pantry, she heard what everyone was saying and went cold all over to find that we'd heard her too. But then she heard Aunt Alex telling Uncle Hugh not to be medeval and getting worked up, so when Uncle Hugh came in to ask her if she'd heard, she couldn't confess what had happened and had to say no because she'd been teased by Aunt Alex before and wasn't going to get into that kind of fix again. And I don't blame her.

———◆———

10

I'm Not Sorry

"Now you get away from here," said Greg testily. "You'll get everything all crumped and gronculated the way you always do when you fuss around. Some foul and random thing will happen."

He was working on a long chart of the Egyptians that would fold up into his book, a chart blocked off into columns, one for each Egyptian age, with small, clear, precise drawings of the divinities scattered around at certain points. The two great gods, Ptah and Serapis, stood on guard, very tall, one at each end of the chart. Anubis, the jackal, was conducting the dead to their underground abode, and Thoth, the baboon, also a god of death, was keeping records of the dead and of the gods. There was Bast, the cat god; Athor the mother goddess with the head of a cow; Horus, the sun god with his golden disk;

and Nut, goddess of the sky, arched over the earth supported by Shuh and Tefnut, gods of the air.

It was all very beautiful, Julia thought. She was in awe of the chart—it was the best thing Greg had ever done. In a more benign mood he had explained the figures to her, but now he seemed nervous and touchy as, carefully—very carefully—he drew over his penciled-in shapes with India ink, shapes he filled in with bright colors as he went along. Occasionally he scratched out a bad line, then groaned when he had roughened the paper, because if you did that, Julia knew, the watercolors didn't go on smoothly.

"I do *not* always crump and gronculate everything," she said indignantly. "I'm a sensible, responsible person. Dr. Jacklin said so." She was feeling especially sensible and responsible because now, at the end of two weeks, she had her last weeding payment wrapped in a little package to put at her mother's place at dinner. And she had almost paid her bill, but not quite. Perhaps she could do something for Dr. Jacklin later on.

Now Greg began whistling under his breath as he worked, and presently he stretched and was silent. "Whatcha reading?" he said. He always wanted to know what people were reading.

"*Girl of the Limberlost.* Now be quiet—" Julia hated being interrupted in the midst of a special book.

Greg picked up the other one she'd brought from the library and left on the dining room table near where he was working. "*The Trail of the Lonesome Pine,*" he murmured and, when he'd flicked over a page or two near

the end, " ' "No, Jack, not that—thank God. I came because I wanted to come," she said steadily. "I loved you
when I went away. I've loved you every minute since—"
her arms were stealing about his neck, her face was up-
turned to his and her eyes, moist with gladness—' Oh,
puke, puke, puke," said Greg.

"Now you shut up, Greg Redfern. I don't keep on at
you when you're reading—you and your old pyramids and
mummies."

"Well, at least Cleopatra never said anything sickening like that. She said,

> Give me my robe, put on my crown; I have
> Immortal longings in me: now no more
> The juice of Egypt's grape shall moist this lip:
> Yare, yare, good Iras; quick. Methinks I hear
> Antony call—

That's what *she* said."

Julia stared at him. He'd spoken the words in such
dark and somber tones, in such an unfamiliar voice, so
different from his usual one, that she could hardly believe it was Greg. It was the deepness of it that had made
a shiver run along the backs of her arms.

"Who was it said that?"

"Cleopatra, queen of the Egyptians, just before she
poisoned herself."

"Was it true?"

"Yes, even though this is a play. She let an asp bite
her on the breast."

"What's an asp?"

"A snake."

108

At once Julia saw the patrician hand clasped about the snake's head as it was lifted and laid in her bosom, the sudden dart of that flat, enameled head set with cold yellow-green eyes, the narrow red tongue flickering out, the gasp of pain, the head drawing back, and the almost invisible mark left on the white flesh.

"Did she—was it agony?"

"Of course. It was snake venom—"

"Say some more, Greg."

"I can't except, 'I am fire and air,' and that's all I remember."

Julia watched him as he went on with his work. Perhaps that's what Jennie was, fire and air.

Julia had set the table only at one end because Gramma said there was no reason to disturb Greg at the other where he was still busy with his bottle of India ink and pens and brushes and glass of water and box of watercolors. There was plenty of room. The little package of coins was at Mrs. Redfern's place, and she was just home from work and in the bedroom changing her dress.

"Gramma," said Julia, bringing in napkins and the sugar and milk from the kitchen, "did you know that a cat's markings on its face are called its mask? Dr. Jacklin told me that, and that Siamese cats are terribly independent, even more so than most cats. And he says they're the most inquisitive cats there are and probably the most intelli—"

"Oh, Dr. Jacklin! Dr. Jacklin! Dr. Jacklin!" cried Gramma, exasperated, and she gave a swipe at the side of her face as if driving away gnats. Yet what she could see were only floaters, they were called, but she never could remember that, even though she knew the dancing specks were in her eyes. They drove her mad, she said. "Dr. Jacklin! First it's earthquakes and now it's him and his three confounded cats. I can't stand cats anyway, and to have to hear about them day and night and Dr. Jacklin says this and Dr. Jacklin says that—I'm at the end of my patience, and that's the size of it, and don't want to hear another word on the subject."

Mama came in and undid her package and kissed Julia, then got the bill and marked it paid and gave it to her. "Now we're all squared away," she said. "I'm proud of you."

"But I still owe you fifty cents."

"No. You've worked hard in this hot weather, and I'm very pleased—"

"Well, I'd let the child finish out," said Gramma. "That's my opinion, though I know you won't pay any attention. Come, now, Greg, don't let your dinner get cold."

But Greg kept right on working, seeming not to hear.

"Mother," said Celia Redfern when they'd begun to eat, "I have something to tell you. I've finally done it— what I should have done long ago, asked for a raise. And it's been agreed on, so now I can begin to hunt."

Julia gazed at her. She could scarcely believe it—it was too good—*too good.* And she looked at Gramma, who hadn't said a word but was just sitting there. And Greg raised his head; his eyes, with a light in them, met Mama's for just the flick of a second.

"But, Celia," said Gramma, "you don't need to. You know that. What do you think I—I mean, you still have money owing—"

"That's right," said Mama airily. "But we'll find something not too elegant," and Julia knew what she meant. Something for as little as possible. Oh, imagine—imagine: she and Mama and Greg hunting for their own place! "Mother," said Celia Redfern, "aren't you pleased? We're impossibly crowded. I'm ashamed—we've stayed too long—"

"But the house will seem so empty," said Gramma in a shaken voice, and she turned to Greg and gave him the strangest look, as if it might be for the last time, then her eyes went down to his chart and studied everything he had there, laid out on the table. But suddenly her face brightened, a glow spread over it and she looked across at Mama. "It'd be far easier to find an apartment with one bedroom for what *you* can pay."

"But, Mother, we'd have to have two bedrooms at the very least. You know that."

"Of course I know it. I mean leave Greg here with me," and all at once Gramma was very busy breaking up a slice of bread and buttering one of the pieces. "He'd have your room, all to himself, with that big desk in there his father made, and all his books and things out of storage."

"Why, *Mother*—"

Julia felt her face, her whole body, suddenly go furiously hot. "Why, that's *my* desk! You know perfectly well my father made that desk for me—"

"There'd likely be no room for it," said Gramma, eating and not looking at Julia. "Besides, what need have you got for it yet, a tyke like you. But Greg—"

"Mother, listen to me. I will not leave Greg—we are a family, the three of us. We'll find a place—"

"But I wouldn't mind, Celia—I wouldn't mind. Greg and I'd get along just fine, wouldn't we, Greg? It's not just because I'd be lonely, but because we get on. We've always gotten on, haven't we, Greg! And I'd be here—not like you, working. Don't you see? That way, you'd get a better place, not having to pay for another bedroom. And I wouldn't mind his things around—I never have," said Gramma excitedly, her eyes, her whole face shining as if she could just see Greg and all his possessions here in her house to stay. "And then I'd still cook—you know I need somebody to cook for. I never do for myself—I can't abide eating alone, and that's the size of it. I can't be bothered—"

"But Greg will not have my desk—"

"I don't want your old desk," burst out Greg in a strange, tight voice. "Who ever said I wanted your old desk—"

"Gramma did—it's what she meant. And you do! Gramma wants you to have everything. If you spread your things all over the place," said Julia breathlessly, "it's just fine. It's part of your work and we have to eat around you. But if I have my things spread out, it's all got to be cleared right off, because it's a mess—"

"Julia—Julia!" said Mama.

"—and if you come in here in Grandpa's wheelchair with a shawl over your head and scare me stiff so that I

112

scream and scream when you wheel yourself toward me with your hands up inside the shawl and all shaking and your face in the dark so that I can't see who it is, Gramma bawls the daylights out of me. But then she looks at you and laughs and laughs because you're so funny and should be an actor. And if you don't like somebody and won't come in, it's because you're busy and have other things to do. But if *I* won't come in, I'm oozing or sulking and making everybody embarrassed. And you can sit and do what you like all day except for delivering your papers or doing a tiny little bit of gardening out in back, but I have to get up and do whatever Gramma wants even if I'm reading or writing in my ledger—it doesn't matter— and that's the way it is, isn't it, Gramma—"

"Julia!" commanded Mama, and reached over and took hold of Julia's arm and shook it, but Julia flung her away.

"You just don't like me, do you? You'll be glad to get rid of me, won't you—because of my father—because you have never—never—"

And had to stop because she had lost her breath entirely. And Gramma, her face covered with little red splotches and her eyes fixed on Julia, suddenly looked over at Mama and with a wide, unexpected gesture like a spasm, as if she washed her hands of Julia, of all Julia had been so unfairly saying, shot out her arms. Her left hand hit the sugar bowl, and over it rolled, right against the glass of paint water, and over *that* went into the bottle of India ink. And the water sluiced like a little river right across Greg's chart, and the ink blended in with it but made its own black lane across Nut, the goddess of heaven, and Shuh and Tefnut, before it reached the river of paint water making its way slowly down across Anubis and Thoth.

"Oh, *Greg*—" whispered Mama.

But Julia couldn't speak for horror—at the devastation, at the expression on Greg's face. He couldn't seem to take in what had happened. And Gramma gave a cry and started up out of her chair and reached over as if to stop the water and ink. Then her hands went up to the sides of her face and she stared at Julia, her eyes glistening with rage.

"Look what you've done—ruined—absolutely ruined—after all Greg's work—" and put her trembling hands over her mouth and burst into tears.

"Why did you?" said Greg in a low voice. He got up, not even bothering to stop the advance of mingled water and ink but let it slide on until it dripped over the edge of the chart onto the floor. "Why did you have to go and say all that?" And suddenly in one furious movement he caught up his chart and tore it into pieces and flung the pieces on the table and went across to the door and opened it and went out and banged it behind him.

For a long time, while the voices went on and on in the other room, Julia lay on Mama's bed in the dark, cater-cornered, just as she'd thrown herself face down when she'd first come in, closed the door, and never even turned on the light. She kept seeing Gramma's white splotchy face while she, Julia, said everything she felt about her and Greg, and that strange way Gramma's arm had suddenly darted out. She saw, again and again, the sugar bowl tilting, knocking into the glass of paint water, and that knocking over the bottle of ink, and the spreading ruin of Greg's chart.

And his face—everything had seemed to stop while she stared at Greg's face, and then Gramma said it was Julia's fault, and Greg said, "Why did you?" looking at her, not at Gram who had done it, "Why did you have to go and say all that?" (And why had she? She hadn't known, just before it happened, that all those violent words were going to come spilling out.) Then saw, as if it were happening in front of her eyes as clear as clear could be, Greg tearing up his chart, filled with fury, as if he hated what he had done—but, no, what she had done, and he would never forgive her. He would act as if she didn't exist, and they would have to go on year after year living in the same house.

The door opened and let through a slice of light, and Mama came in and closed the door again and went over in the dark and pulled up the window. "It's stifling in here, Julia, how can you stand it—" then turned and came to the bed and sat down and leaned over her, laying a cool hand lightly on Julia's face. "Come and tell Gramma you didn't mean what you said—"

"But I did!" said Julia passionately. "You know it's true—"

"Yes, in a way. But she can't help it, any more than Uncle Hugh can help favoring you. Oh, darling, she's so miserable—if you could only—"

"But I don't care about her—"

"Julia, you do—"

"I don't—I don't. It's Greg who matters. Where's he

gone? Why hasn't he come back? And why did he say I'm to blame for what Gramma did? She had no right—"

"I know she hadn't. I told her that. And she keeps saying that if you hadn't turned on her, she'd never have swung out her arm. She said she was so upset. Julia, the poor little woman. You have no idea—she's beside herself for what she did. She can't bear it—she was so proud of Greg's work. Can't you understand that? She had to find some way out, so she blamed you. And her eyes have been driving her mad lately, and the heat. Won't you go out and tell her—"

"Tell her what? Tell her what? That I'm sorry? When I'm not? When I didn't do anything?"

"But if you could just say something. It won't bring back Greg's chart. If you could just go out and say—" And Mama sat there in silence because, Julia thought, she didn't know what there was to say. Julia lay still, thinking the whole thing over and how hopeless it was.

"I'm not sorry," she said after a while. "I said exactly what was true, and she had no right making Greg think I was to blame. I'm only sorry about Greg and all his work for nothing." She got up and took off her clothes and got into her pajamas and crawled into her own camp cot bed. And Mama sat there on the edge of the other bed and said nothing.

Sometime later, Julia woke in the night and asked if Greg had come back and Mama said no, that he was staying at his friend Bob's. She fell asleep again, then woke with the blowing of the wind. It hummed across the roof and whistled under the eaves; she could hear something banging and then a trash can blew over. A bush scratched and scratched against the side of the house; dry leaves were being whisked madly along the street. She stared into the dark for how long she didn't know, twisting and turning, and turning back, and there was a smell like incense in the air as if someone far off had built a bonfire.

11

Up at the Indian Rocks

The wind was still blowing.

Julia peered out from the bedroom to see if Mama was having breakfast, because she had no intention of going out and facing Gramma alone. She listened. Mama was in the bathroom, and she could hear little faint crackling noises in the kitchen and stole out to look.

It was Gram at the sink intent on trying to peel the shell from a hard-boiled egg. But the shell wouldn't come, only in maddening little bits that tore chunks out of the egg. Suddenly Gram threw it in the sink. *"Damn!"* she cried. *"Damn—damn—damn!"*—and snatched up the others she'd been working on and smashed them after it, one after the other, in a fit of such frustrated fury that pieces flew up all over the tile and even onto the window. And just as she had last night, she let out a great gasp like

a sob, then went blindly across the kitchen and out to the back porch, and Julia heard the screen door slam.

"Gram," she whispered. "Oh, *Gram*—" Never in her life had she heard her grandmother swear, nor ever once seen her waste food, turn on it and deliberately ruin it.

School was let out early. Mrs. Gray said in class that a forest fire was raging back in the hills that couldn't be stopped and Julia noticed groups of people standing out in front of the stores along Shattuck, talking and looking off to the northeast at the clouds of smoke boiling up behind Oakland. The sky was dull, the sun coppery, so that it shed an unearthly light and it seemed very small as if it had retreated behind the pall of smoke. The hot, harsh wind, filled with the smell of burning, blew along behind her and there kept being smuts on the backs of her arms and when she wiped them off they left streaks. Charred bits lay all over the sidewalk.

When she got to the music store, Mama was out in front with Mr. Stanhope, standing near Victor, the big black-and-white papier-mâché Victrola dog. He was put at the entrance every morning and brought in every evening and he had his head on one side as if listening sensitively to strains of music no one else could hear. When she put her hand on him he felt gritty. Everything she had touched that day had felt the same: a terrible day, hot and dry and windswept, full of black grits.

"I don't like this wind," Mama said. "I don't like it at all. If only it weren't for the wind—" As she spoke, a fierce gust swept by, rolling an old newspaper and a piece of box top over and over, and here came a hat and an old man stooping along after it. But every time he put his hand down the wind whipped the hat away, so Julia made a dash and pounced on it, and handed it to him.

"I'm going to Dr. Jacklin's," she said. Mama was turning to go in—not thinking about her but about the fire, Julia knew perfectly well.

"Where?" she said. "Oh, up there—I wouldn't, dear. Why not just—?" and she went on in with Mr. Stanhope, who was always trying to get Julia to call him Uncle Phil, and Julia didn't hear the rest.

"But I'm not going home!" she called after them. "I want to go to Dr. Jacklin's. I have to, and I'll be back by closing time."

She had to because she must ask Dr. Jacklin what to do about Greg, who couldn't stay away forever. And she must tell him how strange it was, strange beyond belief, that here at last they could really go and hunt for a place of their own and she had thought she would burst with joy if that day ever actually arrived. And now it *had* arrived, but Fate had twisted everything. That was the strange thing, that quick twisting; everything changed in the space of a breath, less than half a second, when Gramma's hand shot out.

She would go up there and talk to him, and if he was very busy she would go in under the house among the ferns and talk to The Three Mung-gows. And perhaps after a while Dr. Jacklin would come out with lemonade and cookies the way he always did, along about four, when he got tired of working at his desk.

When she got to 226, she knew at once, as she turned in under the arch, that Barty had been watering. She could smell the dampness, the cool, rich, soaked earth, and reached up and pulled down two big sycamore leaves and pressed one to each side of her hot face. She went up slowly, snuffing the wet green smell, delicious after the reeking wind and, listening, heard among the calling of the jays and trolling of the blackbirds that quick bright spilling of notes, like a bracelet of water flung into the air, that was the house finch's song. He was the brown bird, Dr. Jacklin said, with the pinkish-red throat and face, the bird she had freed in the bush when he had got his foot tangled in a hair. Was it the same one singing now? She could never see him, though she had looked.

The instant she came out onto the court, she had a feeling, right off, that Dr. Jacklin wasn't at home. It was all too neat—nothing was on the picnic table but innumerable flakes of ash, and when she looked up, there were The Three Mung-gows sitting at the window all in a row looking down at her. As she stood watching, Timka got up on her hind legs, her front paws resting against the glass, and stared intently at Julia, her mouth opening again and again. Then Sookie and Nanda talked, the two of them walking back and forth nervously in a way Julia had never see them do before, as if they were trying to tell her to come up and let them out.

She ran up the steps to the porch, but knew even before she rang that no one would answer. She climbed around to the back door—but it was locked; all was silent except for the steady blowing of the wind that made a surging sound in the trees like ocean surf on the shore. She could look in through the long windows of Dr. Jacklin's study with its mysterious paintings on the walls and, beyond, into the windows of his bedroom. All was peaceful, with delicate shadows whipped about in the wind, moving on the matting and across Dr. Jacklin's bed, but the sunlight in between the patterns was orange. The very air was orange and ominous.

She turned and went down again, and when she came into the courtyard, Barty was there.

"Where's Dr. Jacklin, Barty? Will he be back?"

"Don't know. He's gone up to the fire station on Grizzly. I'd say he was worried."

"Look," said Julia, pointing to The Three Mung-gows who were standing at the windows, talking, looking down at them with a peculiar intensity. "I think they want out, Barty. Could you go up?"

Barty looked and clapped his old bent claw of a hand across his mouth. "Forgot! Forgot! And after what Dr. Jacklin said." He gave himself a blow on the side of the head as if he deserved it, sprang up the steps, got out his keys, unlocked the door and went in and closed it. Julia waited, expecting the Mung-gows to be let out immediately, but nothing happened. She stood there watching, and saw them turn toward Barty as he entered the living room. Then he did the oddest thing. He did not even look at them, but stood with his hands on his hips studying first one painting and then another. Was he trying to understand them? Next he scratched his head, stood thinking, then turned away and didn't come back.

I know what I'll do—I'll go up and meet Dr. Jacklin and if I don't see him, I'll just come down again and go to the park until it's time to meet Mama.

Behind Dr. Jacklin's there was a little winding path that, after a block or two, led out into the wild hills where there were no houses yet, a path that led over to the right on the way up to Grizzly Peak. But even though the path went up through groves of eucalyptus and oak and manzanita, it was hot going and Julia's eyes stung in the smoky wind. And when she came to the broad meadow and to the rocks as big as houses, she turned from the path, intent on going into a little canyon to find a stream that issued from the hillside and that in the rainy season came down in a rush. It would be cool in among the rocks—she could get a drink and put her feet in the water.

The stream was much diminished at this time of year, but in among the oaks and protected by the overhang of rocks from the sun, the water was still cool. Julia lay beside it and put her face in and came up dripping. She put her lips down and drank, and noticed patches of moss, green and damp as in spring, on the undersides of boulders. There were little ferns and clumps of miner's lettuce clinging to the edge of the stream and, in the middle of it, growing up among bronze rocks and pebbles on its floor, bunches of watercress that shivered and moved with the almost invisible current. It was a delectable place. She pulled some of the watercress and began eating it, rolled over on her back and looked up at the bulging surface of the gray, yellow-lichened rock that loomed over her head. Here, Dr. Jacklin said, the Indians used to come and build their campfires. Perhaps that dark patch, like an enormous outspread hand up the side of the rock, was the mark of their ancient smoke.

She closed her eyes and fell fast asleep.

12

Something Not Remembered

There again—that quick, bright spilling of notes. What were they like? Yes, a fling of water—but where was she? The burning smell—it was eucalyptus; she recognized it at once—was strong, much stronger now. But why? Her eyes flew open. She was in the hills. How long had she slept? She sat up, listening, and heard a crackling, driving roar as though some insatiable hunger were at work. She scrambled up and went and stared out across the meadow that lay just this side of the first sharp climb on the way up to the fire tower. Flames amongst rolling clouds of smoke were leaping from the valley that lay between the rise ahead and the final ascent to the peak.

She took one look and turned and ran, ran, ran. On the steep places she stumbled and fell, bruising and bloodying her knees, but never noticed the hurt, fell again and rolled, got up and ran, slid and rolled and ran

again. Uncle Hugh—he'd said that on Market the fire
raced the people and beat them, took them in, swallowed
them and they vanished. Trees explode with heat.
Eucalyptus explodes, filled with oil, and pines and manzanita, in the dry summer hills.

When she came to the houses behind Dr. Jacklin's,
she turned from the path leading straight down behind
his street to run toward the park, away from the fire that
by now must be racing over the crest and down this side
of the hill beyond the meadow where the rocks were.
She came to the back of the park and for the first time
turned to look where she had been. Flames had just
topped the crest and now the wind had changed and
was driving them down toward the homes beyond Dr.
Jacklin's. She could still hear the roar and, down below,
the wail of sirens. If the wind changed again, driving
them toward her as it had been doing, his house and all
the others by the park would be gone.

The Mung-gows. Surely Barty had let them out. But,
staring up at the pictures as he had done, he couldn't
have been thinking about them. He'd paid no attention
to them. At once, instead of running on down through
the park, she turned back toward Live Oak, and everywhere people were bringing out what furniture they
could carry, and lamps and rugs and clothing, and piling
them in the street or into cars, and other cars were driving
off, loaded with possessions.

"Little girl," called a woman, making frantic motions,
"little girl—come and get in—we'll take you. You must
come away—" but Julia would not turn her head. She
kept running and when she got to Live Oak and rounded

129

the corner, she saw Dr. Jacklin along the block just coming down through the stone arch with something in his arms.

On both sides of the street men and women were desperately packing their cars, or hastening away on foot, carrying all they could manage, and Julia made her way among them to get to him. It was pictures he had, and he put a big one and three small ones against the wall while he tried to adjust another under his arm together with a roll of something. Then he turned and caught sight of her, his eyes widening with shocked amazement. "Julia, where've you been? What in the name of heaven's happened to you? You look—"

"But didn't Barty tell you? I told him I was going up—oh, no, no, I didn't. I went up to Grizzly Peak to meet you—or I almost did, but I got so hot I went in among the rocks and fell asleep, and when I woke up the whole valley on the other side was on fire—"

"Up below Grizzly? My God, Julia—!"

"It's coming, Maury," shouted one of his neighbors, about to drive off. "Hurry—the wind's changed again—it'll be here in no time—I wish I could take you, or the pictures—"

But Dr. Jacklin waved him away. "Doesn't matter," he shouted back. "I'd rather hang on to them and I can make it faster on foot—"

"But did Barty let out the Mung-gows?" persisted Julia. "I couldn't tell. He only looked at the pictures—"

Dr. Jacklin had gotten another roll out of the shrubbery just above the top of the rock wall, and Julia saw that it was a roll of canvas, cut out of its frame. "Can you take two of the small pictures, Julia, and hold them flat resting on your arms so that you can put this roll on top? Barty phoned my sister and she came and got the cats and she and Barty packed up as many of the paintings as they could and took them away—"

"But I can take more," said Julia. "These aren't heavy—let me take that one too." They started down the street, Dr. Jacklin edging her ahead of him through the accumulation of furniture "so that I won't lose sight of you." Julia could hear the murderous crackle up there and the heat had increased with the change of wind. But she wasn't afraid, for some reason, she remembered afterwards, now that she was with Dr. Jacklin and intent only on being able to hang on to the paintings he had entrusted to her.

They turned down beside the park and kept going, very fast, not saying anything, until Julia had to stop when her burden had grown heavier than she could have imagined it would. They stood for a second or two, looking back to where, in amongst the trees bursting into flame four or five blocks above them, Dr. Jacklin's house would be—or would have been only minutes ago. Nothing now but fire and air, thought Julia and looked up at him. His face, with its deep creases, was unreadable. She could not imagine what he was thinking. Did he look sad? But the folds of flesh over his eyes, as well as the creases down his cheeks, had always made him look sad.

They turned and went down, and after a while a man stopped them. "Dr. Maurice Jacklin?"

"Yes."

"Dr. Jacklin, I'm Haze Winkler of the *News*—you may

have read my column. Are these all of your paintings or have you lost some in the fire? I believe you had quite a collection, Picassos and Cézannes, and some by Degas and Monet. Did you save them all?" Now he was moving down the street with them.

"My gardener managed to bring down quite a few—"

"So then you've lost some?"

"Yes, I have—"

"I see you've cut some from their frames but not all—"

"Yes, I'd got home from the fire station up on Grizzly after my gardener and sister had left, and began cutting them out as the easiest way to carry them, but then knew I wouldn't have time to cut all the rest. So I just rolled these up and grabbed what framed ones I could carry and got going."

"And your home is lost by now?"

"Yes, along with everyone else's up there. Now, if you'll just let us go on—we're tired and these paintings are confoundedly heavy. We'd just like to get to where we're going—"

"You have a helper!" said Mr. Winkler, smiling at Julia across Dr. Jacklin. "And may I ask your name?" When Julia didn't answer, "Dr. Jacklin, just one more question," and Winkler moved in a trifle closer, "how does it feel to have lost the treasures of a lifetime? Your collection of paintings has come to be worth a fortune, and there were your manuscripts and books and your record collection. Just what are your emotions at this moment when you realize that everything—"

Julia saw Dr. Jacklin's face change. It hardened and

his eyes brightened. "If you'll excuse me, please," and he went on ahead so quickly that Julia had to skip to keep up, and when she glanced back she saw the man shrug and turn away, and the crowd came in between.

"How did he know everything about you?"

Dr. Jacklin didn't answer for a moment, as if he were thinking. "It's his business to know," he said finally. "And he was just doing his job, but I'm not obliged to lay out my private feelings for everybody to take in with the morning coffee."

They went on, stopping to rest now and then among the refugees streaming down from the hills, pushing baby carriages and wheelbarrows packed with belongings. Julia's arms ached with the weight of the paintings and just when she felt she could not carry them another block, they came to Miss Cora Jacklin's house and there she was with Barty, watching out in front, and when she saw them she clapped her hands together in relief and came running.

"Maury—Maury! And here's Julia!" She and Julia had met once or twice when Dr. Jacklin would bring out refreshments in the late afternoon, and his sister had come by. She took the paintings from Julia, and Barty came and took Dr. Jacklin's. "We wanted to go up in the car again, Maury," she said, "but the police wouldn't let us, and I don't think we could have got through anyway— past all the people. They're roping everything off up there, the police told us, and they're about to start d—" An explosion finished the word.

"Dynamiting," said Barty. "To try to make a fire break."

"Well, it won't do any good," said Julia. "Uncle Hugh told me. They did it after the earthquake in San Francisco when everything caught fire, and they blew up one big home after another, and it wasn't the least bit of use. It just spread the flames."

"But they must do something," said Barty, "or the whole of Berkeley'll go up. The police said there's no more water." He turned and headed for the car, parked in the driveway, to stow the paintings away with the others.

"Maury," said Miss Jacklin, "what are we to do? Just get in the car and go?" Dr. Jacklin looked up toward the fire, the flames almost obscured by smoke. "Barty and I haven't brought furniture out," she said. "I couldn't see a bit of use putting things outside. Why is everybody doing it? If the fire comes, it'll take everything in its path."

"We'll not leave yet. The dynamiting may make a difference. If it doesn't, I'll drive the car further down." Dr. Jacklin lifted his head. "Listen! The wind—it's dropped." Yes, there was a hush, so that for the first time all that could be heard was the murmur of the people going past, talking in low voices to one another, and every three or four minutes another explosion. "Let's stay out here and watch."

Despite the fact that the sky was not to be seen for the roiling clouds of smoke, Julia had all at once a sickening sense of late afternoon, the time just before evening. "Miss Jacklin, what time is it?"

"Why, I don't know, dear. I haven't thought of time—and I haven't my watch—"

Dr. Jacklin looked at his. "Your mother!" he said. "It's six-thirty. Go in and phone—"

"Oh, but I promised—I promised I'd be back at the store to go home with her and they close at five-thirty. I told her I was going up to your place. She'll be—"

Miss Jacklin took her by the shoulders and led her up the steps and inside the big shadowy old house into an enormous entrance hall. "There you are, dear. Sit right down and phone the store. I have a feeling they're there waiting for you."

"But I can't remember the number—I can't remember anything." Circumstance was closing over her like quicksand, because what if Mama wasn't there—what if she was out hunting for her in all that crowd of people. "I could phone Gramma—" but appallingly, she could not even remember, in this shocked instant, what their home number was.

Miss Jacklin had immediately tried to turn on the lamp, failed, and was looking in the phone book over at the door. "Here we are," and she read out the music store number and Julia gave it to the operator.

At once Celia Redfern, as if she'd been sitting right there at the phone all along, answered "Julia?" in a high, wild voice.

"Oh, Mama—yes, it's me. Oh, I'm so sorry—"

"Julia, where are you? Oh, thank God—I thought—because you said you were going up—" For a moment she couldn't continue, then got the better of herself. "Where are you?"

"At Miss Jacklin's—she lives down near Shattuck. The fire hasn't gotten here yet, but the wind's died and they're dynamiting, and the flames aren't so high. We can't see them much anymore. Mama, shall I come—?"

"No, no—the streets are seething with people. The whole place is a madhouse. Uncle Phil and I will try to drive along Shattuck, but if we can't make it we'll walk up. But you stay right where—" and the line went dead. There was no click; simply silence.

"We got cut off," said Julia.

"Try again—" but when Julia jiggled the hook and listened, there was nothing.

"I see," said Cora Jacklin after she had tried, "the lines have gone. No water, no telephone, no light. Well, it's to be expected. What did your mother say?"

"That I'm not to budge. I'm to stay right here, and they'll come and get me."

"But if the wind gets up again and we have to go—"

However, the wind did not get up again, and the dynamiting continued. And they realized after another hour that they would not have to go, because the dynamiting had made a fire break and the wind seemed finally to have fallen for good. In the dusk a vast rosy glow was reflected down from the hovering overcast of smoke— the smoldering embers of Berkeley, acres upon acres reduced to ashes sending up their last light.

Here and there random flames still flared, feeding upon what had not been quite consumed and then one could catch glimpses of the spectral stalks of chimneys pointing up out of the ruin. But the rage, the devouring fury was over and now suddenly the refugees wanted to go back, to see just what had happened to all they'd left, to see if anything could be found, some trinket, some jewel, some metal box of papers or even, miraculously, perhaps larger objects. And the tide of men and women turned, then came to a halt. Barty was right; the fire area was cordoned off now. No one could enter.

"But why not—why not?" demanded Cora Jacklin in indignation. "Not back to their own *homes*?"

"Because," said Dr. Jacklin, "the police can't possibly keep track of who should be up there and who shouldn't. There'll be a lot of thieving."

Miss Jacklin thought that now she and Julia could go and fix something for them to eat while Barty and Dr. Jacklin unloaded the car and brought the paintings inside. And just as Julia, down on her knees, was busy hugging The Three Mung-gows, let out of the kitchen at last where they had been shut for safekeeping, voices were heard outside and here were Mama and Greg and Mr. Stanhope. And Gramma, in her next-to-best dress and her black flat-topped straw hat.

Julia flew to let them in, remembering just in time to watch out for the Mung-gows—for what if they should try to get back up to Live Oak?—and got everybody inside while keeping the Mung-gows away. And Gramma said that of course she was here. Why on earth should Julia be surprised at that?

The minute her daughter had called home, she said, wondering if Julia had forgotten to come back to the store after all, and found she wasn't there, Gramma had decided that what with the fire up in Dr. Jacklin's neighborhood, and Julia having said she was going up there, and what with the masses of people flooding down over the campus and along Shattuck Avenue, she'd go out of her mind if she stayed in that house a minute longer. So she put on her hat and went off to the music store and had been waiting there about half an hour when Julia phoned. And what, she'd like to know, had Julia been up to all afternoon?

So they went into the living room and gathered around while Julia took them, her battered knees in full view for evidence, through every step of her journey from Dr. Jacklin's up into the hills and down again, not forgetting a single incident. She told them how beautiful the room in the rocks had been (hideous now, flashed into her mind, the stream wiped out and the big rocks of rough gray, with yellow and pale green patterns of lichen on their sides, nothing but blackened hulks sitting up there in the devastation) and how she'd bathed her feet and washed her face and rolled over on her back eating the cool watercress, then fallen asleep—

"*Asleep,* Julia!" cried her mother in horror.

"Yes, asleep—and I must have slept for hours. Well, maybe two, and something woke me, I don't know what. Maybe it was the smell of burning, all those eucalyptus and pines and firs on fire, or maybe it was the roar. You can't imagine—that close! Right on the other side of the ridge from where I was—I'll never forget the sound of it. Now I know what Uncle Hugh meant. Now I know exactly what it was like for him. And if I hadn't—"

"If you hadn't waked up," said Greg in a sepulchral voice, "you'd be—right this minute—nothing but a—"

"Nothing but a charred corpse," said Julia.

"Julia!" said Celia Redfern angrily.

"That's right," said Gramma, matter-of-fact. "You foolish, foolish girl. The hand of God, that's what it was, reaching down to pluck you out of your danger when you knew good and well there was a fire in the hills and a wind blowing. But you went up nevertheless, flinging every iota of common sense to one side, as if you positively wanted to finish yourself off."

Now Julia grappled them to her again with the story of her descent from the hills, telling how she fell time after time until she thought her legs must be broken and the pain was something terrible; how, because she was determined to save the Mung-gows, she refused to be taken down by car when everyone around her was trying to get away as fast as they could; and how she and Dr. Jacklin just barely managed to escape the jaws of that ravenous monster, though they could feel its hot breath not five minutes away. "Isn't that right, Dr. Jacklin?"

"Well, yes, it is, Julia, though I'll have to admit I hadn't thought of it in quite that way—"

Just barely managed to escape with six more of the paintings in frames, Julia swept on, and she didn't know how many rolled ones, and then a newspaper reporter had stopped them, wanting Dr. Jacklin to tell the readers just exactly how sorrowful he was over having lost his treasures.

At this point Gramma seemed suddenly to behold the will of the Lord in a different light—not rescuing, but punishing—and ended Julia's story by saying, "The hand of God, that's what it was—this fire. And I can't make out why. I don't know what the people of Berkeley have done to deserve it, the way I could make out about San Francisco. But we can't always perceive into things like this. We're not given. But you don't get a holocaust like this one without some reason behind it," she said ominously.

"It could possibly have been a dropped match, not put out, was the cause," suggested Dr. Jacklin. "Or possibly a campfire left burning. What with the wind."

"No, no, I mean something deeper than all that," said Gramma. "There's some reason, I tell you—some reason—" and she went on slowly shaking and shaking her head.

Julia rose up on her camp cot that night, her pajamas soaking with perspiration. She'd dreamed she hadn't wakened in time, that when she'd opened her eyes from her nap in the hills, the Indian rocks were surrounded by flames.

She got out of bed and went over to Mama, but she was deep asleep, Julia could tell by her breathing. So she went quietly back, then saw a line of light under the door into the hall and knew that Greg was awake too and probably reading.

He *was* reading, sitting up with his own pillow and a couple of sofa pillows behind him and a glass of milk in one hand and a sandwich in the other, and his book on his knees. This was one of the things he enjoyed most in the world, reading in the dead of night with something to eat (he was never really *not* hungry) and everyone else fast asleep, everything quiet. "Hey," he said, looking up. "Whatsamatter?"

Julia came over and sat down on the edge of his pull-out bed. "Greg, I had the most awful dream—"

"That you didn't escape, you mean."

"Yes."

"I know. I have them like that, and that's when I get up and get something to eat and start reading. It helps."

"Greg—" and she sat there, not quite knowing what it was she wanted to say. He waited for a second or two, then left her to her own thought. What had it been? Something about being up there in the rocks, waking up. Yes, she'd had a feeling, just this minute, that it hadn't been the smell of burning that had waked her, nor the sound of the fire. Well, those could have been the reasons and she might not have realized it. But it seemed to her now there'd been something else, something that had seemed very strange to her, strange and wonderful in the fleeting instant it had stayed in her mind when she'd gone out and beheld the fire leaping up toward the crest of the hill.

13

———◆———

A Letter to the Paper

Julia had the Tuesday, September 18, 1923, paper laid out in front of her on the dining room table. FIRE SWEEPS BERKELEY, she read. And underneath, *Fifty Blocks Razed; 6000 Left Homeless*. She went through every word of how scores had been treated at hospitals for burns from embers dropping from the sky and for other injuries, and hundreds of homeless refugees were gathered on the campus, and 7500 fire fighters, including 5000 university students, and thousands of other citizens "had thrown their forces into the battle and rallied to victory." She read every name of the owners of private houses destroyed and the list of known injured, and came to a list of the missing. She ran her finger down—and there was "Redfern, Julia"!

She stared up in amazement at Mama and Greg and Gramma. "But I'm *not* missing. What do they mean?

Look, right there—" and she took the paper around to show them. Then it dawned on her: for the first time in her life she was in the news. She was thought to be missing, and everybody would know.

"Oh, that," said Gramma. "As soon as I got downtown and heard people giving out names of children they couldn't find, I gave yours. I thought it best to do whatever I could even if you did turn out to be found."

Now Julia sank down with the paper again, bent on absorbing every last paragraph, and here on another page, embedded in a long report of the regular columnist, Haze Winkler, she found Dr. Jacklin's name. "Everybody, listen to this! 'Dr. Maurice Jacklin, retired professor of Art History at the University of California, told this reporter last night that he had lost many of the fine Impressionist paintings he has been collecting ever since he bought his first Cézanne when the painter was not yet famous.

" 'Not only his paintings, whose worth he did not reveal, but his extensive record collection, as well as his valuable collection of art books and all of the manuscripts of his own publications, have been destroyed in the fire. Dr. Jacklin and an unknown child—' why, that's me again," exclaimed Julia. "Maybe I should have given my name, but I just didn't feel like it." And after reflecting for a moment on her own perverseness which had deprived her of further fame, " 'Dr. Jacklin and an unknown child,' " she continued, " 'were carrying away what they could of the paintings from his burning home. His gardener, Mr. Barton Williams, and his sister, Miss Cora Jacklin, had rescued several of them some time earlier.

" 'Later, in another interview last night, Dr. Jacklin revealed that he does not intend to rebuild on his property at 226 Live Oak Lane for at least three years while the garden is replanted and growing again. He plans meanwhile to return to France to the village he and his wife lived in during the time they were beginning their collection of Impressionists.

" 'His wife, Ellen Jacklin, whose wishes and ideas Dr. Jacklin had carried out in the plan of their home, died three years ago. As Dr. Jacklin stood in the crowd fleeing from the burning area during the first interview, looking up to where their home and garden had been not half an hour earlier, there were tears in his eyes. He seemed heartbroken.' " Julia couldn't believe it. "Why, he did *not* have tears in his eyes. You couldn't tell *what* he was thinking. He did *not* cry."

And she went at once and got her ledger, tore out a page, wrote a highly indignant letter to the newspaper, and mailed it herself the next morning on her way to school.

When she got home that afternoon, Dr. Jacklin telephoned from the music store to ask if she minded her name appearing in the paper as the one who had helped him to bring down his paintings. He hadn't told the columnist because he'd thought Julia didn't want her name given. She said that now she didn't mind, and told him how sorry she was that he was going to move away and would he be taking the Mung-gows with him? Yes, he would, and she was to be sure to come and say good-bye to them and to him, too. She had written a letter, she said, to that columnist last night putting one thing straight about the interview, and had mailed it this morning. Dr. Jacklin chuckled and said that, as a matter of fact, it was exactly what he was doing at this very moment.

Two days later their letters appeared together in the Editor's Mailbag section of the newspaper.

> Dear sir: [said Julia's letter] I could hardly believe my eyes when I read in a column of your paper that Mr. Winkler saw Dr. Jacklin cry when he looked up to where his house had been. He did not cry and I know because I was the unknown child who was with him. He is not a crying sort of person. He wasn't feeling sorry for himself. I think you should apologize.
>
> Julia Caroline Redfern

Directly underneath was Dr. Jacklin's letter.

> Dear sir: I was somewhat taken aback on reading Haze Winkler's tale of my weeping as we stood talking on the evening of the fire. It is quite true that I lost a number of treasured possessions but then so did 6000 other people, and I did not see anyone crying about it. We were all of us filled with sorrow, but I noted particularly the stoicism with which most of my neighbors packed up what they could and made their way down the hill. I did not feel in the least like crying, nor did I while speaking to your columnist, or at any other time.

146

I do not think it at all unseemly for a man to weep, but it was not as if I'd lost a loved one in the fire.

My companion was Miss Julia Redfern, aged 11, who appeared at my house in the nick of time. If it hadn't been for her, several more of my paintings would have had to be left behind because I couldn't have managed them. I am more grateful to her than I can say, and to my sister, Cora Jacklin, and to my gardener, Barton Williams.

Maurice L. Jacklin

Beneath Dr. Jacklin's letter was the following reply:

I do indeed apologize to Dr. Jacklin for the misrepresentation of his emotions given in my September 18 column.

Haze Winkler

14

<hr/>

Space for a Desk

Uncle Hugh couldn't get over Julia's letter in the paper. He was delighted with it.

"Well, but it was just what I knew," said Julia. "I had to write."

Uncle Hugh and Aunt Alex had come across in their car on the auto ferry to see some friends of theirs who had been burned out. Aunt Alex, now that the weather had turned cooler, had on a perfectly cut rose-rust suit, a small close-fitting hat set slightly to one side on her smoothly brushed hair, and there were pearls at her ears. She looked, as she herself would have put it, "absolutely smashing."

On this Saturday afternoon Julia and Mama and Greg, as soon as Mrs. Redfern could close the store, were going to look at an apartment she had heard of, and when Aunt Alex and Uncle Hugh dropped by on their way

back to the ferry, Uncle Hugh said that of course he
would take them. What was more, he wanted to see this
apartment himself. Whether or not Aunt Alex was over-
whelmed with eagerness to see it wasn't at all evident,
as she said nothing to Uncle Hugh's proposal.

She sat there quietly, one knee crossed over the other,
on the typist's chair at the desk where Celia Redfern,
whenever she had a chance, typed out bills as well as
letters of reminder concerning unpaid ones; sat there and
gazed up at the enormous framed photographs along the
walls of famous opera singers with hands clasped under
jeweled bosoms in the case of females, and across rotund
stomachs in the case of males.

Julia had already given Uncle Hugh a full account of
all she had been through when he had telephoned the
day after the fire. "—but what I don't understand," she
was saying now, "is why the flames didn't gallop down
and engulf us all the way they did in San Francisco
coming along Market. You remember, Uncle Hugh, you
told me they raced the people and beat them—"

"Well, of course the wind took a different direction in
your case," said Uncle Hugh. "And then also I think it
was the high buildings along Market that did it—fifteen
and twenty stories one after the other—so that there was
a positive canyon of flame the whole length of it—"

"Do you know something?" said Aunt Alex. "I have
by this time heard more than enough about the fire. It
was all the Morrises could talk about."

"But, Alex," said Uncle Hugh, "of course it was all
they could talk about. It was a frightful experience and
they have very little left but the clothes they stand in.

And it was why we came over, after all, to talk to them."

"Yes, I know. But I *have* heard quite enough." Aunt Alex opened her purse, got out her compact, and powdered her nose. She smelled delicious, Julia thought, not obviously so, but there were occasional heavenly wafts. And when she replaced her compact, Julia watched her fingers with their immaculate rose-colored nails shut the purse with a rich click and felt a twinge of pleasure at the sight. She couldn't imagine why certain sights, certain sounds, unimportant as they were, did this to her.

Uncle Hugh parked in front of the shingled house. It had a graveled drive along which, a little later, Greg and Mama and Julia and Aunt Alex and Uncle Hugh followed in the wake of a very small lady in a peacock green dress who wore her white hair piled on top of her head and whose name was Mrs. de Rizzio. The driveway led back to a lawn bordered on the right by a broad bed of roses. On the other side was an aviary where canaries flew back and forth, up and down, from perch to perch and occasionally let out bursts of song. In back of the aviary was a high hedge of Scotch broom which, Julia found afterwards, enclosed a wild shrub garden. On the lawn was a swing with striped cushions and a striped top; Aunt Alex headed for it and settled herself in comfort.

Mrs. de Rizzio went over to the porch of the apartment near the aviary and unlocked the door, and Greg and Julia stepped inside into a living room with two windows along the back and a big one at the end that looked out under an oak tree into the wild garden. Mama and

Uncle Hugh stayed on the porch talking to Mrs. de Rizzio.

Julia knew there was an upstairs and she had seen a balcony as they came around the corner. "Oh, Greg," she said in a tense voice.

"Do you suppose," he said, "there'll be enough room for the three of us?"

When Mrs. de Rizzio came in with Uncle Hugh and Mama, she explained that there was a kitchen, not very big, out there by the de Rizzios' back porch; a room across the hall from the living room which Greg, with all his books, might like; upstairs a larger bedroom for Mrs. Redfern, and a little room with two big windows and a balcony that might be right for Julia.

"Would it have space for a desk?" asked Julia.

Mrs. de Rizzio smiled and her eyes twinkled as if she'd heard about Julia's desk. "Oh, I think so," she said. "The problem, I imagine, would be getting it up those narrow stairs."

She left them so that they could explore, and Uncle Hugh and Greg went immediately to examine the room that might do for him, while Julia and Mama went upstairs, Julia leaping ahead. They came out into a burst of light. For there was a well that had been built up from the hall below that became a glass well as it ascended through "Julia's room" to the roof, where it was covered by a frosted pane. There was glass in the door opening into the big bedroom, as well as in the door opening onto the balcony. There was a skylight in the sloping roof "right over the place where I'll have my camp cot," Julia decided at once, "so that I can look up at the sky." And

the two big windows along the garden side, to the right of the balcony door, were each made of four large panes and opened outward.

"Mrs. de Rizzio said they'd thought of this as a sun-room," said Celia Redfern. "That's why it's so small—it wasn't really intended for a bedroom."

Julia stood in the middle and turned, taking it all in. She noticed that there was a square door about waist high on the side where she'd have her bed, and she went over and opened it. It was all dark in there and smelled of warm wood, and she could hear someone moving around on the other side of a wall to the left. The de Rizzios' bungalow was single story, but this apartment, built on behind, was two stories. So that of course what she was looking into was a part of their attic, and someone must have an attic bedroom. "I could keep all my stuff in here," she said contentedly to herself. "It would be per-fect." She turned and faced Mama. "Absolutely perfect."

They studied one another, then Celia Redfern went into the other room and wandered about, looking out of the windows, and turned and came back when Uncle Hugh appeared at the top of the stairs.

"Oh, Hugh—I don't know, I don't know. I shouldn't—the rent's really more than I—"

"But I'd like you to have it, Celia. Don't worry about it—we'll work something out."

Julia stared up at him. She'd never once thought of him in connection with this decision. "Oh, Uncle Hugh—"

And here came Aunt Alex up the stairs. "What's this—what's this?" she called out. "Be careful, Hugh." There she was, smiling at them, and then at her husband, sending him at the same time, Julia noticed, a little quick, warning, married look. A message. "What with all the work to be done on your mother's house, remember, while she's away, and sending her to England and outfitting her to go—and I didn't tell you, did I, Celia, that I'm off to Europe for three months, and we're having our place redone, painted and papered, and the draperies and rugs cleaned throughout. Hugh'll join me for at least a month when it's finished, and we'll come back to everything fresh and shining. You know how I loathe disorder, so I thought it best to just—" Aunt Alex lifted her shoulders and gave a wave of the hand "—go away."

"Alex," said Mama, "I never had any intention—"

"Oh, I know, my dear. I know. It's just Hugh. He can quite lose sight of reality sometimes. Unwisely generous, you might say," she explained, just as if Uncle Hugh weren't there. And before anybody could say a word, she'd lifted her head, nodding approval. "This is to be Julia's room, of course. Charming. Perfectly charming. But where's Sister to sit, Julia? On the bed?"

This was too much and Julia refused to answer, then before she could stop herself, "*No*where—" she shot out furiously.

"Oh, you little wet hen!" laughed Aunt Alex and ruffled her hair.

Julia had used to have an ever-present companion when she was small and Greg, at eight, refused to be tagged around by a six-year-old, and Julia warned Aunt Alex one day where Sister was sitting. But Aunt Alex only said, "Oh, Julia—you and your imagination," and plumped her big behind right down on top of Sister.

Now Aunt Alex moved away into the other room. "And this would be yours, Celia. I love it! It has all kinds of possibilities, what with these large windows opening right out into the trees. I always say that if you have trees, nothing else matters—"

Julia looked up at Uncle Hugh. His face was flushed, set, with that tightness around the eyes more noticeable than ever. In fact, Julia thought, he looked utterly unlike himself.

"Hugh," said Mama in a low voice under what Aunt Alex was going on about in the other room, "Hugh, you know I would never accept—"

"I will do what I plan to do," he said, then touched her arm and turned and went off down the stairs, quickly, without a word, and Julia ran down after him. When he got to the bottom he twisted round and glanced up at her. "Bye-bye, Julia," he said. "You go back up, now. You and your mother have things to settle." Yes, he wanted to be by himself—he didn't want to talk to her or to anyone. And there would have been nothing to say—it would be so embarrassing after what Aunt Alex had reminded everybody—who was the boss. She hesitated, then went on down and gave him a firm hug and a kiss. His cheek felt hot.

"Goodbye, Uncle Hugh." She waited a moment in case by some chance he wanted to say anything, but he crossed the little hall to put his head in to say goodbye to Greg, then went out through the living room and the front door closed behind him. Julia could hear Aunt Alex upstairs, giving advice in her clear, carrying voice.

"You'll want pale yellow silk in here, don't you think, Celia? Right to the floor, and a sweep right across these two windows on the long side so that the wall won't look cut up. Oh, I can just see how my draper would do it—"

Julia went in with Greg. He was stepping off measurements and singing absentmindedly to himself the little song Gramma always sang when she was busy and content,

> Tori chee, tori cha,
> Papa's in the cunjee house,
> Mammy's in the lavwasar—

or so it had always sounded to Julia.

"What's a cunjee house?" she had asked. "What's a lavwasar?" But Gramma hadn't a notion.

When she came in, Greg looked up at her. "Do you suppose it's all a joke?" he said. "When I was a little kid I thought the world had been put around everywhere as a joke on me—put there specially."

"But what was really here, then?" asked Julia.

"That's what I wondered."

"But why you? Why a joke on you? As if you were the only person in the world—"

"Well, as I said, I was just a little kid." He was quiet for a bit, looking all around the way Julia had upstairs. It was a big room, rather shadowed, which somehow seemed right for Greg, and there would be plenty of space for everything. He could build lots of bookshelves. "What does Mom say?"

"She can't decide. She says the rent's too much, and Uncle Hugh said he wanted to help and then Aunt Alex came up and said, 'Now, now, Hugh—' or something like that and told us how unwisely generous he is without even looking at him and embarrassed us all horribly and that's why he wanted to get outside." She thought for a moment. There was something she wanted to say to Greg, and it was because of Aunt Alex doting on him, and Gramma too. She didn't really want to bring it up for fear of ruining everything, yet somehow she had to. "Greg, what about your chart? I couldn't help it about Gram—"

"Oh," he said, "I'm going to do it all over. I never did like the way I was scuffing up some of the drawings when I rubbed out a wrong line. You can't do it—it's hopeless. I asked an art teacher about it and she said to put the drawings in in pencil, then do the watercolors, and it doesn't matter if you go out over the pencil lines. After that you do the outlining in ink, free and easy, and I know exactly what she means. I've seen ink and watercolor done that way—nothing tight and careful. You have to know exactly what you're doing." Now another thought came to him, but having something to do with the chart. "I told Gram I'm not going to stay with her there—that I have to go with you two."

"What did she say?"

"She tried to persuade me and I felt like an ungrateful clod."

"But, Greg, if you stayed with Gramma she'd wait on you hand and foot. You'd be the center of everything even worse—I mean, even more than you are now."

"I know. And I didn't think I could take it."

Now they heard Aunt Alex's heels on the stairs and in a second or two she looked round the door. "Ta-ta, you two. My poor old Hugh'll be wondering what on earth has happened to me. Good luck, darlings. If it's right for you to have this apartment, you'll have it. Don't worry—!" and with a ravishing smile and a special little wink for Greg, she went clicking away across the bare and echoing floors and the front door closed again.

Greg and Julia went upstairs and there was Mrs. Redfern standing at one of the big windows looking out and thinking, perfectly still, not seeing what she was looking at, Julia knew.

"Being inside the house of your head, aren't you, Mother?" said Julia.

Celia Redfern didn't answer, then finally, "Yes—yes, I am." Julia stood watching her, wishing with her whole being that she would decide the right way, for if they could only move here it would be the happiest time of their lives. They couldn't possibly, now, live anywhere else. It was unthinkable.

Mrs. Redfern turned and looked at Julia—and Julia looked back, holding her breath. "Julia, when you want something, you press so hard—you have no idea."

"But I didn't know—I didn't mean to. I haven't said anything."

"You don't need to. You want things so passionately you don't need to say."

"But it's up to you, not Julia," said Greg.

"Yes, of course, and I've thought it all over very care-

158

fully, and I think we must take it. At least we'll try, and if I've made a mistake and can't manage, we'll move."

But Julia had an idea that once in, they would not move. Somehow they would manage.

15

Goodbye, Julia

Julia, for the last time, was at the Woollards' door. She just wanted to say goodbye to Maisie, she said, because they were moving. Maisie came and looked out, standing beside her mother but coming no further.

"Yes, I've heard all about it," said Mrs. Woollard. "And I hear Greg doesn't want to stay with his Granny. Seems to me it wouldn't have hurt him—the poor old lady, there all by herself at her age. Goodness knows what could happen to her."

"But she was there by herself before we moved in," pointed out Julia. "And Mother thought the three of us should stay together, and besides, Gram's going to visit Aunt Flora in England the way she's always wanted to and she's excited about it, even if she won't admit it."

"Ah, yes, well," said Mrs. Woollard, "I suppose the

situation just wasn't convenient for your mother any longer."

Julia didn't like the sound of that at all, whatever it might mean. "But we have no room—any of us. And my mother says Gram and I aren't temper'mentally suited."

"That I can *well* believe," said Mrs. Woollard, lifting an eyebrow and looking off over Julia's head. "Though a child can always be made to behave. But I suppose we must all of us resign herself to being left alone whenever our children choose to leave. Now you get back here, Maisie Woollard," she said, just as if Maisie was about to light out for good this very instant. "Down to the end of the block, and five minutes, mind. Supper'll just be ready."

Maisie and Julia got away down the back steps quickly in case there should be more conversation and instructions, raced along the side of the building but, once out in front, went along at a leisurely pace.

"We saw your letter in the paper," said Maisie. She'd heard at school, along with the other children who hadn't had any fire adventures, all about Julia's narrow escape and the saving of the paintings. "Mama said she thought it was impertinent of you to say that the newspaper man should apologize. She said that wasn't for a child to say."

"Well, but he *did* apologize. And he might not've if I hadn't written."

Maisie reflected on this. "But there was that other letter—the one from the man."

"Well, they might not have believed just him," said Julia. "And I was there. And besides, I didn't know he was

161

going to write. Maisie, did Gramma tell you that I paid my mother every cent—well, almost every cent—for that pan?"

"Oh, yes," said Maisie, looking tired. "We heard all about it, how you weeded and weeded and weeded day after day in the hot sun and earned the money. Your grandmother was so proud—you should have *heard* her." Julia was astounded. "She was so proud," went on Maisie, "that my father said he didn't see but what you were only doing what you should have."

Julia was filled with bitter indignation. "Well, I like that!" She stopped in the middle of the sidewalk and glared at Maisie. "*You* ruined the pan, too— *you* were part of the whole thing—*you* were the one who said let's get a pan out of the pot cupboard. I like that! I didn't see *you* earning any money to help pay back— *I* did the whole thing!"

"Yes, but you didn't get spanked."

For an instant or so Julia weighed getting spanked against two weeks (off and on) of weeding. Actually, she'd never much minded being spanked because it only lasted a minute. It was the weight of everybody's hard feelings she really couldn't put up with. That was the worst. As for the weeding, if she hadn't, she'd never have met Dr. Jacklin and the Mung-gows and had all those happy times. Well, of course, then she wouldn't have got into the fire, either. But then—*then* she wouldn't have been up there to help save Dr. Jacklin's paintings. On the whole, she thought, her glare dying away, she'd really come off much the best, weeding or no weeding.

She walked on. "Maisie," she said, "do you realize we might never see each other again—never, never?"

"Why not? We'll both still be at the same school."

"No, we won't. I've found out I'll be going to another one."

Maisie didn't say anything for a little. Then she shrugged. "Well, anyway," she said, "I've got lots of friends."

Yes, that was true. Ever since school had begun, she'd been running around screaming with everybody at recess, and here at home, Julia had seen, the other afternoon when she'd come home late from school after being kept in for failing her arithmetic test, Maisie having the best time with the neighborhood children. Mostly she and Maisie had kept to themselves after school, as long as they'd known each other, making up their own games and imaginings. They'd never seemed to need anybody else. But Maisie, Julia knew all at once, would never lack for kids to be with.

About herself she couldn't be so sure. She'd be in a new neighborhood, she realized fully for the first time, and at a new school, and felt a sudden sinking, a scared coldness. She'd been so taken up with the idea of her room, how she'd arrange it, that she hadn't thought about this. But it would be all right—it *would*. Her room! Her room! She wouldn't need anybody. (Oh, yes, you will, Julia Redfern—always one person, one friend, at least.)

"I wish you could see it, the place we're moving to, Maisie. And the room I'm going to have. It's upstairs, with a balcony where you can look out over everything. And

Greg's going to garden for the de Rizzios—those are the people who own the apartment and live in front—so he can earn something and help my mother."

"Oh? And what are you going to do?" said Maisie.

Julia was stopped. "Well, I don't know yet. Maisie, maybe you could come on over when we get settled and I get my room fixed. Do you suppose you could?"

"You know I can't. You know perfectly well my mother'd never let me."

Yes, Julia did. Julia was "a thoroughly bad hat," as far as Mrs. Woollard was concerned. Hopeless. For instance, what if Julia had persuaded Maisie up into the hills with her and they hadn't gotten out? She could just imagine Maisie taking home the story of Julia's thoughtless venture into the hills, her falling asleep—and her waking, by the merest chance. "There you are! What did I tell you!" Julia could hear Mrs. Woollard exclaim. "You simply can't trust that child—"

They stopped at the corner of the vast field that separated their two houses, the field they'd run over day after day, before the mouse episode, to get back and forth to visit each other, and that Mama used going to and from the streetcar that crossed the train tracks. Now she and Julia would know this field no more.

It was damp, gray, late afternoon with a curious arrangement of dark, steely-edged clouds out there beyond Gramma's house where the bay was and more wide fields with the cows in them where she and her father used to walk, and Greg too sometimes, to get down to the wharves on Sunday. Now the sun, like a molten eye peering out, was sinking below them toward the shadowy earth and sending its rays straight across the fields so that Maisie, as Julia studied her, was bathed in its rosy-copper light.

"Well, then, Maisie," said Julia, "I guess we'll just have to say goodbye."

"I guess we will," said Maisie, and the words came out as neat and compact as her lean little body, her smooth head, her still-clean dress and unwrinkled stockings and tightly done up shoes. "Goodbye, Julia," and she turned, trotted back along the block without lingering, twisted round once to wave, and continued on her way. Julia watched until she disappeared.

So that was that about Maisie. They'd been friends ever since they were six. Julia started slowly across the field and for some reason thought of her father and the dream she'd had about him the other night. She was back in the brown bungalow where they'd all lived together, but it had nothing in it—no furniture, not a single thing. And she heard her father talking, but when she went from room to room hunting for him, he was not there. She heard him, yet the house was empty. She was alone.

Now Jennie was gone, too, and Gram was going to England, and Julia and Mama and Greg were moving, and she might not be going to see Maisie ever again, nor maybe the Mung-gows and Dr. Jacklin. Who knew whether they'd be coming back from France? His house was gone, and the garden, and all those houses up there— she looked up at the gray and black ruin lying in a swathe across the other side of Berkeley—and so that woman's house was gone, the kind woman who'd come out with Dr. Jacklin's records when Julia thought she'd lost them.

All so strange—so strange. Everything changed in so short a time. And this was something she'd thought of while she was with Maisie: how if it hadn't been for cremating the mouse she'd never really have gotten to know Dr. Jacklin, because if she hadn't had to earn money for the pan, she'd never have stayed up there to weed for him.

Oh, but on top of that—and she stood looking at the wide sky from which the gray was fleeing inland leaving it a powerful evening blue except for those curious dark clouds over there above the crimson sun—now, at last, something had come to her full force. She remembered— she *remembered:* after she'd rescued the bird caught in the bush by a hair tangled round its leg, and had gone up to Dr. Jacklin's and told him about it, he said that a brown bird with coppery-red on its head and breast was a house finch. Then when she heard the rippling, patternless song, he'd said that that was the house finch's, and she was always afterwards listening for it and trying to see him sing.

And when she'd been asleep among the Indian rocks something had wakened her. She'd thought it was the fierce smell of burning or the roar of the fire, but it hadn't been. She remembered. It was that clear spilling of notes. She'd been fast asleep, and there it was, either in her dreams or somewhere around her. She'd come to and smelled the burning and heard the fire, and got up and ran to look out.

Everything was so strange. That's what she couldn't get over—the strangeness, now, of being here, alive, and of everything that had happened. One thing after another. She looked up at the sun—only a small segment of it left above the earth—and she knew: this was what she wanted to call the journal Uncle Hugh had given her: *The Book of Strangenesses.* She would begin writing in it the first night she could sit at her own desk up in her own room, and this would be her private celebration. She would tell about Jennie the way she had wanted to but hadn't yet, and about the bird caught by a hair and how she had held that hot, throbbing body and gently drawn it forth, opened her fingers—and it had vanished almost before she could see it go. And then what Dr. Jacklin had said, and how it had all turned out.

Yes, *The Book of Strangenesses.*

And she went on across the field along the same path where Patchy-cat used to sit waiting for Mama, when she got off the streetcar after work, so that he could trot beside her and keep her company going home.

———◆———

(Continued in *A Room Made of Windows*)